BATTLE OF THE NESTERS

After the Civil War, most of the South went back to normal life, but there was no end to death and destruction for some. Such were the men who had fought with Quantrill's Raiders, self-confessed bandits and killers. Clem Vance was warned that if he rode south into Texas territory after the outlaws who had once fought with the infamous band, he would be heading straight into trouble. But Vance rode on. Could he bring to justice some of the most vicious killers the West had ever seen?

ALEX FRAZER

BATTLE OF THE NESTERS

Complete and Unabridged

LINFORD
Leicester

First hardcover edition published in Great Britain
in 2002 by Robert Hale Limited, London

Originally published in paperback as
Trouble Shooter by Chuck Adams

First Linford Edition
published 2004, by arrangement with
Robert Hale Limited, London

British Library CIP Data

Frazer, Alex
  Battle of the Nesters.—Large print ed.—
Linford western library
  1. Outlaws—Texas—Fiction
  2. Cattle stealing—Texas—Fiction
  3. Western stories 4. Large type books
  I. Title II. Adams, Chuck. Trouble shooter
823.9'14 [F]

ISBN 1–84395–298–X

Published by
F. A. Thorpe (Publishing)
Anstey, Leicestershire

Set by Words & Graphics Ltd.
Anstey, Leicestershire
Printed and bound in Great Britain by
T. J. International Ltd., Padstow, Cornwall
This book is printed on acid-free paper

1

Night Raiders

The rays of the afternoon sun were beating down on Clem Vance like the heat rays from hell as he urged his sorrel into the buttes country. This was new territory to him and although he kept his eyes open as he rode, the narrow trail had so many twists and turns in it that it was only possible to keep track of his direction by watching the sun all the time. The dust from the rocks came up from beneath his mount's feet in little red-brown puffs which hung dryly in the still air, so that his nose and throat were burning with it even though he had ridden less than a dozen miles since sun-up. The bushes that hung listlessly by the side of the trail were covered in a thin red film of dust which gave them a queer, dead-looking appearance.

The only splashes of colour he saw to relieve the monotony of red and brown, were the occasional darting lizard which slid across his trail at intervals, yellow and purple, and, sometimes, he caught a glimpse of the slick grey of a coiled rattler sunning itself on a smooth outcrop of stone. He rode the rutted trail on a wary edge, eyes flicking nervously, alertly, from side to side, one hand hovering ready above the Colt at his hip. The heat of the sun was a stifling pressure on his back, beating into his flesh as he sat straight and tall in the saddle, sunlight tracing flashing rings of fire along the metal loops into which his gear had been lashed.

Senica lay some thirty miles to the west, and around the frontier town lay nothing but desert, until one reached the cattle country a little to the north. It was in this direction that he intended to ride, coming into Senica from the north, scouting the area first before he rode into town. Although he had never ridden this trail before, there was little that he did not know about Senica and the territory thereabouts. It was a barren frontier town, hewn out of the uncompromising land so as to form a natural gateway into the south and east, used by the big cattle drovers for shipping their cattle through, some as far south as the Rio Grande, others by rail to the east.

He took a swig from the half-empty canteen at his side, running the warm, brackish water around his mouth for a moment before swallowing it. His tongue seemed to soak up most of it before it even got the length of his throat. The thick, sharp alkaline taste of the desert had been in his mouth ever since dawn when he had ridden down out of the hills to the east, across the southern edge of the Redstone's east-west traverse, into the harsh country of the trail-blazers and the cattle drovers. Somewhere along the trail, he knew that he had crossed the frontier between east and west, between those places where law and order were supreme, and those in which the law of the gun prevailed. For close on seven days now he had been on this trail, moving westwards, seeing no one, deliberately choosing the desert trail so as to arrive in Senica unnoticed.

The war between North and South had ended two years earlier, with the South still smarting under the indignity of defeat and the North impoverished by the long battle. Both sides had tried to settle down again, to pick up the threads where they had been broken during the war, when families had been divided, brother against brother, father against son. But although most of the men who had been under arms during the war had gone back to their old pursuits, there were still some who could not settle down to a peaceful life.

Men like those who rode with Quantrill, who took orders from neither side, who seemed to have lived simply for the sheer sadistic delight of plundering and killing. Even as he thought of them, something seemed to tighten in his mind and the fingers which closed momentarily on the butt of the colt in its holster, were like rigid bars of iron. Although several of the men who had ridden with Quantrill had been captured, tried and hanged for their deeds subsequent to the war, there were still some hiding out in the frontier country, men with a price on their heads, outlaws and cattle rustlers, selling their guns to the highest bidder, prepared to continue killing provided the price was right.

It had been a bunch of men such as this who had killed Sheriff Peterson in Carson City, the man who had been more than a father to him, who had reared him after his own parents had been killed shortly before the Civil War by a marauding war-party of Indians. He had heard the shooting while inside the livery stables and had rushed out into the street in time to see the bunch of outlaws riding off, leaving three men dead in the dust. One of them had been

Peterson, shot in the back before he had had chance to draw his gun. Kneeling in the dust beside him, Vance had sworn to hunt down the men who had killed him, to bring his own form of vengeance and justice to them.

He swung the sorrel across the harsh, sun-glaring expanse of desert in front of him where there lay only the shimmering, twisting dust-devils and the dry, acrid stench of the sage and mesquite. In the distance, beyond this sun-baked desert, this terrible flatness of red and yellow, lay the township of Senica, the beginning of the trail into the wastelands, and the stamping ground, according to the stories he had been told back east, of the men he had sworn to kill. The knowledge was a tightening thing, churned up inside him by the long, sober thoughts while he had ridden out from Carson City. It was something that had been eating into him like acid through mile upon mile of inhospitable country. Now, it was only a few more miles ahead of him and he had to circle the town so that he might have time to study the situation, to try to assess the danger which undoubtedly awaited him and to try to figure out how the odds might be stacked against him. He had one advantage over these men. He knew them whereas they did not know him and he doubted if they could guess at the deadliness of his intentions. This was an advantage he meant to keep for as long as possible. Even his name would mean nothing to them.

★   ★   ★

The sun was still half an hour above the horizon when Clem took one last swig from his canteen, then pushed it back into the leather holder strapped to the saddle. He had reached the end of the winding trail across the alkaline wastes of the desert and was now in richer, greener country. This was the cattle country which lay just to the north of Senica, the trail along which the huge herds of prime beef would be driven to meet the railroad further to the east. His sorrel was tethered to a mesquite bush and he himself sat in the lengthening shadow of a tall tree. The red ball of the sun was dropping swiftly towards the rearing black mountain peaks far to the west and the short period of dusk in this territory would soon be over. Night was moving in rapidly from the east, spreading a deep purple haze over the sky. The first handful of stars were coming out but there was a moon just coming up and knew that, although he did not intend to travel after dark, it would give him enough light to see by. The air was clear here and cool after the dry pressure of the desert country and he breathed deeply of it, glad of the opportunity to relax for a little while. By lifting his head a little, he could just make out the faint yellow lights of Senica in the distance, but there seemed to be a faint mist over the creek which lay in the direction. He felt more assured inwardly now that he had reached this point without trouble and began to make camp, lighting a fire with the dry brush which lay in abundance around him. He ate his meal of bacon and beans slowly, then wrapped himself up in his blanket, stretching his long, lean body on the cool ground, staring into the starlit heavens for a long moment, trying to compose his thoughts. Nearby, the sorrel moved softly on the end of the short rope. Apart from that, the night was very quiet.

It was still dark when he woke, coming awake instantly, his mind searching for the sound which had awakened him. His hand slipped the Colt from its holster as he rose softly to his feet, eyes staring into the moonlit darkness around him. The sorrel was chomping impatiently on the bit now, moving around restlessly as if it had sensed something out of the ordinary. He stood quite still, every sense stretched to its utmost limit. Then he heard it quite clearly. The sound of hooves pounding the dirt in the distance. Once, he thought he heard the sharp crack of a pistol shot, but he could not be sure. A few clouds began drifting across the yellow face of the moon sending large shadows across the terrain. He hurriedly saddled the sorrel and swung himself up, gigging it forward over the low rise in the direction of the sound. All thought of sleep had now vanished from his mind. It was not usual for herders to move their cattle under cover of darkness if they were doing it legitimately.

Brush along the bank of a wide river gave him cover as he rode forward. The plaintive lowing of cattle was easily discernible now and he was able to gauge the direction from which the sound was coming.

He stretched himself up carefully in the saddle peering ahead. After a few moments, directly ahead of him, some two miles or so distant, he could make out a compact mass of rippling shadow, just visible in the moon-thrown blackness of one of the hills to the west. Out of the corner of his eye, he could just make out some of the men riding the herd, urging it forward. Circling the herd, the men rode to the head of the long valley, the dim moonlight hiding them sufficiently so that it was doubtful if anyone else in the vicinity knew what was happening. Through narrowed eyes, Clem watched the men moving the herd along the trail. They carried out their task quickly, efficiently, and above all, silently. Their purpose was clear even to him. Only rustlers would be moving cattle out like this by moonlight and he judged that there must be close on three thousand head of prime beef cattle in that herd. This was an operation which had been well planned and carried out.

One or two of the older bulls, Clem saw, were far from easy. They kept sniffing the air and moving uncomfortably, as though sensing that something out of the ordinary was happening. It was clear that if those men out there were not careful they could have a stampede on their hands. But there was nothing he could do to prevent this wholesale rustling. These men were prepared for any opposition they might meet on the trail and one man would not be able to stop them.

He reined his mount in the shadow of a looming outcrop of rock as the first wave of cattle streamed past, filling the air with the thunder of their rushing hooves, their bellowing roaring in his ears. He kept a tight rein on the horse as it threatened to shy at the sound, knowing that if he once gave away his presence there, he could expect no mercy from these rustlers. From the shouting, he judged that the men were having difficulty keeping the massive herd moving together and in the direction they wanted. The grey-brown hides of the cattle glistened with a matt finish in the moonlight as they surged past his hiding place in a solid stream. Dust and sand was stirred up by their thudding hooves. A growing cloud of grit hid them from view for seconds at a time. Grass, leaves and stones pounded him as he sat there hunched over the neck of the sorrel, trying desperately to identify the men herding the cattle as they were forced to pass close to him in the narrow valley. A few of the cows and calves reached the end of the valley and then stood there hesitantly, bellowing loudly. Behind them came the younger bulls, eyes wild and white in their heads, black faces and horns lowered as they pushed and thrust their way massively forward, great shaggy humps and foreparts bouldering along irresistibly, allowing no obstacle to stand in the way of their mad, headlong rush.

Clem kept a tight grip on the reins, knowing that if the sorrel took even a half dozen steps forward, into the path of that mighty stream, it would mean the end of them both. They would be caught up by the solid black walls of beef and muscle, thrust down by the sheer weight of meat, and trampled to death beneath those pounding hooves. Then came the last waves of animals, the older bulls of the herd who always seemed to bring up the rear when driven like this. They pounded onward through the narrow valley as old men might move. Louder, heavier grunts ripped from their bellowing throats, steam blowing from their distended nostrils, the smell of sweat stinging the back of Clem's nostrils. In the dust-blown darkness, he caught a vague, fragmentary glimpse of the four men who rode after the herd. They were evidently so confident of themselves that none wore masks over their faces and he saw two of them clearly and knew that his suspicions had been verified. Those were men of the Quantrill band that he had sworn to hunt down. The urge to pluck the guns from their holsters and send a fusillade of shots hammering into their backs was almost more than he could control, but he fought it down savagely. That

14

would be not only a hasty, but a foolish thing to do. He could not hope to kill all of these men and the others would kill him, surely, if he tried to fight it out with all of them. Best to bide his time until it was more in his favour.

Gradually, the thunder of the herd faded into the distance and he rode out a little way into the valley. The yellow dust was beginning to settle and now no longer caught at the back of his throat. He debated the position for a long moment, then decided that it was highly unlikely the rustlers would come back along that trail during the remainder of the night and there was no point in him riding into Senica until daylight.

The next morning, Clem rode slowly up the main street in Senica, eyes alert, his long, lean, brown face burned by the sun, regular-featured from beneath the high forehead hidden beneath the wide-brimmed hat. His square jaw was proof of determination and purpose and the twin guns, hung low, were sufficient warning to anyone who thought to try their chances with this rangy stranger in town.

To the casual onlooker, it would be apparent that he watched everything in view, or tried to, his eyes were not steady, but flicked incessantly from side to side, or up ahead, even behind him whenever he turned his head, as though afraid he might be followed. A couple of men seated on the boardwalk eyed him curiously, as he rode by, then turned their attention elsewhere, obviously dismissing him as just another saddle tramp riding into this lawless frontier town, looking for an easy job, or for trouble.

Senica had obviously seen many men such as Clem Vance, and there was little about him to make him stand out in a crowd. Although it was still only midway through the morning, about half the population of Senica seemed to have retreated indoors away from the swiftly increasing heat of the sun and only a few people were lounging outdoors. A handful of horses were tethered to the hitching post in front of the solitary hotel, creatures with bowed heads, evidently just beginning to feel the full effects of the sun.

In the very middle of the town, he spotted a wagon train, standing in the street, drawn up to one side. A few women in poke bonnets could be seen and a handful of children who ran around the horses and wagons, oblivious of the oppressive heat. Clem gave them only a cursory glance. Homesteaders, passing through the town on their way to the new grounds which had been opened up by Government grant to the west of Senica.

How they would fare once they reached this land, he did not know. He had seen the same kind of thing happen in many places further east as the tide of civilisation had rolled further and further westward, as new territory was opened up by the Government in Washington. The main trouble was that the Government was so far removed from this frontier country that they knew little of what was actually happening here. The big cattle bosses wanted none of these homesteaders. Whenever they came, their first task seemed to be the throwing up of barbed-wire fences across the trails, parcelling the land into small blocks which they tilled and turned into corn land. By barring the trails, and open ranges, in this way, they made it difficult for the trail herders to get their beef through to the railroad and gunfights inevitably flared up, often into a full-scale range war. Whenever that happened, a lot of people were bound to get hurt and it was in situations such as this that the gamblers and outlaws made their richest strikes.

He reined his mount and sat for an idle moment in the saddle, in front of the Sheriff's office, eyeing it curiously. It was impossible to tell how his information would be received by the law. There had been instances, when the Sheriff was merely a paid hand, working hand-in-glove with the crooked cattle bosses and if that were the case here, honest people would stand little chance of a fair shake of the dice.

Swinging his lean body out of the saddle, he hitched the sorrel to the post, fingered the guns in his belt absently for a moment, then walked into the office, easing the door open gently and almost thrusting his way inside. It was cooler inside the office and the two men sitting there regarded him coldly as he stood looking from one to the other.

'Either of you two gentlemen the Sheriff?' he asked politely.

The older man behind the desk gave a quick nod and drew him an appraising look which seemed to take in everything. 'I'm Sheriff Ellison,' he said flatly. 'Looking for something? You look like a stranger to Senica?'

'Just rode in,' he affirmed. His gaze flickered from Sheriff to the other man seated in the chair. Younger than Sheriff Ellison, he guessed him to be a half-breed with some Indian blood in him. The smooth sallow features held no expression and the eyes were empty, like those of a rattler. A dangerous man, reflected Clem, and tried to place him. But the face was unfamiliar, and he did not think that this was one of the men who rode with the outlaws he had come so far to find.

'I camped out to the north of town last night,' he explained. 'Saw something there you might be interested in.'

Something rose and fell in the Sheriff's eyes. His smile grew wintry beneath the drooping black moustache. Clem saw the quick glance which Ellison threw the other man and wondered what lay behind it.

'Reckon I know what's on your mind stranger,' said the half-breed thinly.

'Let me handle this Gomez,' interrupted the Sheriff harshly. He looked up at Clem, his mouth tight. With an effort, he managed a smile. 'Just what did you see, Mister?' He leaned forward, resting his elbows on the top of the desk.

'Somebody got plumb away with about two thousand head of cattle last night,' went on Clem quietly. 'They took 'em through the valley and headed south into the desert. Probably they're headed clear for the border right now.'

'Did you recognise any of the men rustling them?' Ellison asked.

Clem shook his head slowly. 'Never saw any of them in my life before,' he muttered. 'Though I'd probably know three of them again, if I ever caught up with them again.'

The Sheriff let go a tight, meagre smile. 'We heard about that rustling episode early this morning. The Double-O ranch lost nearly a thousand head. The rest came from the Running-W spread. Lucky you didn't tangle with those hombres, Mister. If you had, you wouldn't be alive this morning. They're killers, every last man among 'em.'

'Then you know who they were?'

Clem eyed him sharply.

The Sheriff's eyes held little patience and there seemed to be rather more of worried just below the surface. He looked to Clem to be an honest man, sober and conscientious, capable of forming judgments quickly but inflexibly. On the face of it, Clem felt sure that the other was not in the pay of the lawless elements in this territory, but there had been some occasions in the past when he had thought the same thing, only to discover how wrong he had been.

'They were outlaws, my friend,' said the half-breed Gomez smoothly, blandly. He sat easily in his chair and regarded Clem with a sardonic smile playing on his thin lips. 'There is scarcely a single ranch in the territory that hasn't lost a thousand head or so in the past few months. The rustlers strike during the night and drive the cattle south into the desert and then over the border a hundred miles or so to the south. More than a dozen men have been killed in gunfights with them.'

'They why don't you git together a posse and ride out to capture them?'

'That's easier said than done, stranger.' There was a vague dryness in the Sheriff's tone. The muscles of his jaw lumped and his fingers twitched a little where they rested on top of the desk. 'No one knows when or where they'll strike next and it ain't easy to get together a posse to fight men like that. They're all professional killers, gunslingers from out east. Some say that they fought with Quantrill in the war. Be that as it may, they seem to be able to strike whenever and wherever they want to. Once they get a herd of cattle together, they light out for Mexico. Then they show up again when they're least expected. All I know, is that they're reputed to be the fastest gunslicks this side of the Mexico border.'

'And why are you so interested in them, stranger?' asked Gomez softly. His gaze was hard and speculative. 'Do you intend to stay around here and perhaps capture them yourself, to claim the reward? If you do, then take my advice and forget it. There are ten men up on Boot Hill right now who tried to do that. They fancied to get themselves a little reward money, but it didn't do them any good.'

'But somebody has to stop 'em. They can't go on terrorising the territory for ever.'

The Sheriff looked him over a trifle sadly and the black moustache seemed to droop even more pronouncedly than before. 'You look pretty handy with those guns of yours,' he said slowly. 'If you want to git yourself killed though, that's your affair.' He lifted his head swiftly as another though struck him. 'You ain't got nothing agin them yourself, have you?'

Clem felt that he might be able to trust the Sheriff, but as far as the half-breed was concerned, he wasn't quite so sure. He paused for a moment, then shook his head. 'The only time I ever saw 'em, Sheriff, was last night in the moonlight when they drove that herd of cattle through the valley and almost trampled me down. Reckon it's just that I don't like being ridden down by a bunch of cows, no matter who's driving 'em. If it's all right with you, I reckon I'll stick around here for a few days, just in case they do turn up again.'

'And if you meet up with them — what then?' queried the half-breed. His lips were curled into a smile of sardonic amusement, 'I know how these men work. They will shoot a man in the back rather than challenge him to a fair fight, even though they are fast with a gun. You'll need far more than luck if you decide to tangle with them.'

'Thanks fer the warning,' said Clem, nodding. 'But I'll keep my eyes open.'

He stepped out into the sunlight again and threw a swift, all-embracing glance up and down the dusty street that slumbered fitfully in the oppressive heat. There was a stillness over everything that he did not like. The town seemed to have a peculiar waiting quality hanging over it as if expecting something disastrous to happen, something over which it had no control. He shook off his dark thoughts, mounted, and rode in the direction of the hotel. If he was to stay here he would need to get himself a room. He turned his horse over to one of the grooms, paused for a moment to see the kind of care it would get, then went into the hotel through the side door, satisfied. A sleepy-looking youth sat behind the large, walnut desk. He glanced up sharply as Clem strode in, then got hurriedly to his feet.

'I'd like a room,' said Clem quietly. He pulled the register towards him, wrote his name and the date. The clerk gave it a quick glance, then nodded as if to himself, reached on the rack behind him and took down a key. 'Second door on the right at the top of the stairs,' he said tersely.

Clem took the key, walked slowly up the narrow stairway, paused at the top for a moment and threw a swift glance over his shoulder. The clerk was watching him out of puzzled eyes, but looked away again quickly when he caught Clem watching him. He pretended to be busy with something at the back of the desk.

Thoughtfully, Clem unlocked the door to his room, went inside, and placed the key in the lock. The room looked out onto the courtyard at the side of the hotel, with the livery stables opposite. There were a couple of horses in the courtyard, in the charge of one of the grooms and he watched idly for a moment as the other led them through into the stables. The room was larger than he had imagined and there was a narrow balcony outside the window. A wash-basin stood in one corner with a large pitcher of cold water standing on one side of it. The bed looked wide and comfortable.

He unpacked his roll, then went over to the basin and washed his face, before sinking down on the bed. Even with the window wide open, the sunlight came shining almost directly into the room and as it was now close on midday, the heat, even in the room, was almost unbearable. As he lay there on the bed, he tried to relax his mind as well as his body, but it was not easy. There were so many thoughts churning around in it which refused to give him peace. There was little doubt in his mind that these men engaged in rustling cattle through to the Mexican border were the same outlaws he had come here to find. But if the Sheriff and the half-breed Gomez had been right, those men would now be halfway to the border and might not return for many days. In the meantime, it was up to him to find out as much as he could about these outlaws, try to find a way of defeating them. More than anything else, he needed help from someone he could trust, but at the moment, he could think of no one who would fit that description.

When he had first set out from Carson City there had been the possibility that these men might have learned that he was riding west to meet them, and he had been wary of an ambush all the way west. It seemed, however, that by deliberately choosing the more devious trails to Senica, he had thrown them off the scent, always assuming that they had known he was heading in that direction. If they didn't, it made things a little easier for him. It meant he still had the advantage of surprise and it was up to him to make the most of it.

He still felt tired after the broken sleep of the previous night and he rolled over onto his side in the bed and closed his eyes. Little sounds came from the distance, making themselves known. There was a drumming of a horse, far away, possibly on the outskirts of town, the throbbing of hooves vibrating through the still, hot air.

A few moments later, he was asleep, one of the Colts held tightly in his hand, almost hidden beneath his body.

When he woke, it was almost dark. There was a gnawing hunger pain in the pit of his stomach as he went down the stairs and into the room at the front of the hotel. The place seemed almost deserted. There were a couple of old prim-faced ladies at the table in the corner who gave him a quick glance then looked away again quickly. He had an impression of white lace and stiff black dresses and then a short, sad-faced man came up to the table and he gave his order.

The meal, when it arrived, was excellent. He ate slowly, realising for the first time how ravenously hungry he was. Not until he had finished the last scrap did he lean back in his chair, sipping the hot coffee.

When he went out into the street again, he noticed that the homesteader's wagon which he had seen when he had first ridden into town was still there and that it had been joined by two others. His glance merely brushed over the small group of men standing beside the leading team of horses, sweating after their long pull through the desert country from the east, then he paused at the sound of angry words. One name that he heard mentioned in a savage, furious voice, stopped him in his tracks.

Turning quickly, he crossed the dusty street to where the group stood in the shadows. A few of the homesteaders, short, sturdy, capable-looking men, carried rifles in their hands and were gathered menacingly around a tall, angular-faced man dressed all in black.

'Now see here, Jason,' snarled one of the homesteaders, his voice reaching Clem clearly as he strode towards them. 'We got title deeds to that land out there and we aim to take it. And neither you nor your boss is going to stop us.'

'I think you'll find that Mark Heller's rights to the land in question — in fact to all of the land to the north of Senica as far as the Tovanatee River — are better than yours and as his lawyer, I think I ought to warn you that if you persist in going through and squatting on that range, you'll be trespassing and here, that means you can get shot.'

'I ain't going to be run off my land by any two-bit cattleman,' hissed the homesteader thinly. He stepped forward, the rifle raised, but Clem moved between the two men and caught at his arm pulling him back.

'Steady, friend,' he cautioned quietly. 'That won't solve anything. You ain't going to help yourselves by getting mad at this hombre. He's just the mouthpiece for Mark Heller. He's the man you want to take your grievances to.'

The homesteader swung round sharply, shaking off Clem's restraining hand.

'And who are you, mister?' he grated harshly. 'You look just like another cowpoke to me. You always stick together, don't you?'

'I'm no cowhand,' said Clem stiffly. 'I'm no nester either. Just don't like to stand by and see people like you running into trouble, that's all. And if you try to set yourselves up against a man like Heller, then you're in for big trouble. That's all there is to it.'

'That's just what I've been trying to point out to these people,' declared the lawyer thinly. 'Mister Heller wants no trouble. But he owns the land out there, in fact most of the grazing land in this territory and no Washington title deeds are going to change that one little bit.' His voice became a little ugly as he went on: 'This is the frontier here and the sooner you nesters and sodbusters realise that the better it will be for all concerned. My advice for all is either to stay here in town, or to turn right round and head back the way you came.'

'But we can't do that, mister,' protested one of the women, pushing her way forward. She stretched out her hands in a slightly pleading gesture and her face seemed grey and haggard in the dim light. 'We've all sold everything we had back east to come out here. The Government promised us the land when we paid for it. We parted with all of our savings to get it. And now you tell us that we can't have it.'

'I'm sorry, Ma'am, truly I am,' said the lawyer. 'But my hands are tied as you can see. I can do nothing about it except warn you against getting yourselves killed by any hasty action you may be deciding upon. Heller has men and cattle on that range out there. Those riders have orders to shoot on sight any nesters who try to force their way onto the land.'

He turned sharply on his heel and walked quickly away, his booted heels clicking hollowly on the wooden board walk.

'If this cattle boss Heller figgers that he can swindle us out of our land like this, then he's mistaken,' snarled the first nester. He checked his rifle purposefully.

'Better do as he says, at least for the time being,' suggested Clem quietly. 'Ain't no sense I can see in getting yourselves killed.'

'There'll be more of us heading into Senica in the next few weeks,' grunted a second man standing near the wagon.

'Once they arrive we'll have close on seventy men here, all ready and able to use their guns. We'll see then if Heller and his hired killers can deprive us of our rights to that land.'

Clem shook his head. 'I still think you're going about this the wrong way.' He watched the women and children as they climbed back into the wagons, the women serious and worried, the children a little wondering, excited by this new turn of events, understanding little of it.

'If you have these land grants from the Government then they'll hold up in court. You have only to take them to the Sheriff, or wait until the circuit judge reaches Senica and put your case to him. Whatever you do, it has to be done legally. Otherwise you'll be playing right into Heller's hands. Then he'll have the law on his side and much as the Sheriff would like to help you then, his hands will be tied.'

'Mister,' said the leader quietly, ominously. 'You don't fool me one bit with this talk of yours. I reckon I can guess whose side you're on. Probably Heller paid you to put this proposal to us when his lawyer failed to scare us off. But I've seen things like this happen before, too many times. The Sheriff will be in Heller's pay, so will the judge. Sure, we'll all stay here in Senica. We'll stay here and rot and be forgotten and the courts will do nothing for us.'

He turned to the men standing behind him. 'If we want our land, land which is rightfully ours, we'll have to fight for it. Once the others git here, we'll go out there and take land by force.' He turned back to Clem, his mouth tight, and looked at him closely. 'And you, Mister. If you are one of Heller's men, then you'd better watch your step. Because we mean to kill any one who stands in our way.'

Clem shrugged. There seemed no point in arguing with these men any further in their present mood. The only good thing was that they would not make any trouble openly until they felt more sure of themselves, until the other nesters arrived in Senica in a few weeks time. Before then, he hoped to have found a way to prevent this inevitable range war and all of its accompanying bloodshed. He did not doubt that these men would fight for their land as they had declared. They had sold up all of their possessions back east to buy these wagons and land and had endured the long and terrible journey out here through some of the most barren country in the whole of the west. Small wonder that they were in such a savage mood and would trust no one.

As he left the wagons and walked through the dusty street, one thought, one name was pounding incessantly through his brain. Mark Heller! The man who had pulled the trigger and had shot down Sheriff Peterson in Carson City. The one man, above all, that he had sworn to kill. But how had such an outlaw managed to buy all of this rich land and become evidently a powerful and influential figure around Senica?

It seemed obvious that Heller regarded himself as being sufficiently far beyond the reach of the law here and felt reasonably secure. He found himself thinking back to his meeting with the Sheriff earlier that day and in particular with Gomez, the half-breed. A dangerous type of man who would think nothing of killing to gain his own ends, or of selling his gun to the highest bidder. How deeply were either of these men in with the outlaws and in particular with Mark Heller?

It might pay him to find that out as soon as possible so as to know just where he stood. In a situation like this it was as well to know one's friends and enemies. Already a plan was beginning to form in his mind. There was danger in it for himself, but he had never baulked at that in the past and he did not intend to begin now. First to discover how deeply the Sheriff and Gomez were in with Heller and then to ride out and take a good look along the trail to the north of town. He also wanted to have a talk with some of the cattlemen who had lost some of their beef to the rustlers.

Making his way back to the hotel, he went up to his room and lay down on the bed, fully awake, staring up at the ceiling over his head, and waited for midnight. Occasionally, he heard the yells of raucous laughter in the streets as the saloons began to empty. Someone fired off a couple of shots into the air. But gradually, silence settled over Senica as the men in Whisky Row cleared out of the saloons and cheap gambling houses.

It must have been a little after one o' clock in the morning when he finally rose quietly, swinging his legs to the floor and getting smoothly to his feet. He checked the Colts in their holsters, then stepped out onto the balcony. There, he eased his way along the outside porch until he was able to drop silently down into the wide courtyard.

The moon was hidden by a long bar of cloud to the south-east, but there were thousands of stars out, gleaming brilliant over his head and affording plenty of light to see by.

The buildings stood out gaunt and silent against the night sky as he left the courtyard and moved out into the main street of Senica, past the livery stables. A horse snickered softly inside one of the stalls as he passed and he paused, pressing his body tightly into the wall for several moments, eyes darting from side to side, alert for any movement. But there was no further sound in the whole length of the street and he worked his way forward, cat-like.

One place, out of all the buildings along the street, still showed a yellow light in the window. It was the doctor's house. Probably, reflected Clem, he was still busy, sewing up some drunk's cuts, even at that early hour of the morning. He edged past it slowly and with caution. Not that he imagined he had anything to fear from the doctor. He could not visualise the other being in Heller's pay. But at this time of night, he would not have welcomed anyone in the street watching his movements.

Ten yards further on, at the corner of the street, stood the Sheriff's office. The place was quiet, in darkness, and looked to be deserted. But Clem was taking no chances. Gently, he eased one of the Colts from its holster and held it tightly in his right hand, finger on the trigger, as he tried the street door. As he had expected, it was locked. Silently, he worked his way around to the side of the building. In the distance, beyond the edge of town, out in the desert, a coyote howled mournfully as the moon eased its way clear of the cloud which had hidden it and flooded the street in front of him with silver.

There was a small door at the side which obviously led to the cells. It too was firmly locked but a window, close by, was open by less than half an inch. Not much, but more than enough for Clem. Swiftly, he inserted the blade of his hunting knife into the thin crack, turned it slowly. The blade bent a little under the strain, threatened to snap with the pressure he was exerting. But the steel of which it was made had been expertly fashioned. He knew its limitations well. A few seconds later, there was a sharp snap and the window moved easily under his hands.

Quietly, he eased his tall, lanky body inside. The passage beyond lay in complete darkness. Cautiously, he went forward, his eyes gradually becoming accustomed to the inky blackness, hand outstretched, groping his way along the wall until he came to a door which was partially open. As he had surmised, this was the door leading into the front office facing the street. One of the windows there was shuttered, the other, however, was not and he pushed the shutters into place before striking a match and looking about him with interest.

There was a paraffin lamp on the corner of the desk and he lit it before the match had burned down. If the Sheriff was in with Heller he would undoubtedly keep any evidence tying him in with the crooked cattle boss well hidden. He searched the room thoroughly without finding any trace of incriminating evidence. It was not until he began to tap the walls of the room gently with the butt of his revolver that he discovered the hollow section directly behind the Sheriff's desk. The safe was well hidden and it was several minutes before he located the small button which slid back the panel in the wall. Inside, by the flickering light of a match, he saw the small bundle of papers and the three large stacks of dollar bills and behind them, tucked away at the back, almost out of sight, a heavy cotton bag. Reaching in, he pulled it out, untied the cord around the neck and looked inside, drawing in his breath in a sharp gasp of surprise at what he saw. He had half expected to find the Sheriff in with the crooked cattle boss — very few law officers in these frontier towns lived long unless they worked hand in hand with the powerful hellions. But the most he had expected was to find that he had been easing things for Heller's men in town without making things too obvious, arranging bail for them whenever they were picked up on any charge, or leading the hastily-formed posses in the wrong direction whenever they set out after the rustlers. But inside the cotton bag were more than half a dozen large pieces of gold. There was no mistaking the precious metal even in that light and he estimated that there was close on five thousand dollars' worth of gold there. Far more than any Sheriff could make in a lifetime of honest work. He tied up the bag and replaced it inside the safe. Now he knew most of the answers as far as the Sheriff was concerned and he had little doubt that Gomez was also in on the deal.

Before closing the safe he had a quick glance through the official looking documents in the safe and what he saw sent a wave of fury through him. They were all land deeds in the name of Mark Heller, witnessed by the Sheriff and Gomez and dated a year earlier. All very clever forgeries which would undoubtedly be used as evidence in any court into which the homesteaders tried to plead their case.

He slid the panel back into place, went over to the desk and blew out the paraffin lamp, leaving the room in darkness. He was on the point of going forward to pull back the shutters over the window he had found open, when he heard the stealthy sound of footsteps on the boardwalk outside, coming closer. There was the faint murmur of conversation from just outside the office.

Very quietly, he moved back into the room, through the door at the back of the room and into the passage, leaving the connecting door slightly ajar. In the darkness, a key rattled loudly in the lock and he heard the door leading into the street being pushed open. Through the crack in the door he could just make out the two, dim shadowy figures standing there, momentarily silhouetted against the doorway and then they had stepped inside the office, closing the door behind them. But recognition had been immediate. Sheriff Ellison and the half-breed Gomez. In a way he had expected them to come back to the office, when none of the decent citizens of Senica would be around to see them.

He pressed his body tightly against the wall of the corridor as the Sheriff struck a match and lit the lamp on the desk. Shadows were thick and huge in the room as he held his breath, listening to every word the others said. There was a creak as the Sheriff lowered himself into his chair, and then the smooth, cold voice of the half-breed said thinly: 'You're sure that this stranger didn't recognise any of the men riding that herd last night? If he was close enough to see the men, he could have recognised them. He said that he might be able to pick them out if he saw them again.'

'Could be,' admitted the other. Clem saw him lean back in his chair, his face etched with shadow by the flickering light of the lamp. 'But he's only guessing in the dark. He knows nothing. If he tries to make trouble, then I'm sure that you can handle him.'

'Of course.' There was silence for a moment, then Gomez went on. 'There's one thing I don't like. He was out there talking to those homesteaders just after Jason left after telling them not to go any further. I think he could make some trouble for us if he stirred them up against Heller.'

Ellison shook his head ponderously. 'They won't do anything. If they do, I'll see to it that any who're left after Heller's men have finished with them are run out of town. We don't want any sodbusters in this territory. It's been cattle country since the beginning and we don't aim to change now.'

'What you mean to say is that if Heller should lose out on this deal, then you will stand to lose everything. Is that not it, Ellison?'

A dark flush spread over the Sheriff's square features. For a moment, Clem thought that he intended to leap out of his chair and draw on the other, but he forced his anger down and smiled bleakly at the half-breed. 'All of us stand to lose a lot if Heller loses this fight. But there's no need for us to worry about that. He's far too clever a man and he has plenty of men to back him up. By now, those cattle will be near the border. The men will be back in a couple of days and I'd like to see those sodbusters go against them, even if they do bring in more wagons in the next few weeks as Jason says they will.'

There was a hard expression on the half-breed's face as he sat back in his chair. 'You're sure that you have all of the evidence in a safe place? Heller asked me to make certain of that.'

'It's safe enough, where no one will find it. If those nesters try to bring their case to court when the judge gets here, we'll simply produce those forged land deeds, all dated before theirs, and they'll be thrown out of court.'

'And with Heller being one of the biggest losers in this rustling business, no suspicion will fall on him. After all, a man does not rustle his own cattle. We might even be able to lay the blame on these sodbusters if they do decide to settle in Senica. Then we ought to be able to shoot them legally.'

Ellison uttered a short, harsh laugh, pulled a bottle and two glasses from the drawer of his desk and placed them on the table, uncorking the bottle with his teeth. He poured two glasses and pushed one towards the half-breed. 'Here's to the continued success of our little enterprise here,' he said quietly. He downed the glass of liquor in a single gulp and poured himself a second. 'And if that stranger does start poking his nose into our affairs, then I'll leave him to you.'

'It will be a pleasure,' smiled the

other. He drank the whisky slowly. There was a note of utter malevolence in his voice. 'As soon as Heller gives the word, that cowpoke is as good as dead.'

2

Polecat Breed

Midday, Clem had ridden out of Senica and taken the trail to the north of the town, keeping his eyes open for any sign of Heller's men who were supposed to be patrolling this part of the range, on the look-out for nesters moving in to squat. Ahead of him, in the distance, lay the foothills of the mountains from which the rivers flowed. Nothing seemed to move as far as the eye could see and there was an ominous stillness over everything as it shimmered in the midday heat. Here, the sun was not as strong as to the south, in the desert country, but it still struck with an uncomfortable heat through his thin shirt and there was sweat on his brow which kept running continually into his eyes as he rode. Clem crinkled his eyes against the glare of the sun and scanned the grass-covered slopes. It was strange, he thought, that he could see no sign of cattle about here. According to Jason, the shady lawyer that Heller had hired, the cattle boss was running a big herd on this grassland.

He reached the river half an hour later and rode slowly along the nearer bank, eyes alert. Usually, when there was a big herd in the neighbourhood, they came down to the water at some time and their hooves made plenty of marks in the mud along the banks, but here there seemed to be nothing like that. Not until almost an hour later, as he topped a low rise, did he see any sign of life. The ranch which lay in the wide, lush valley below him, could belong to only one man — Mark Heller. Even from that distance, with the sunlight gleaming on the walls, it was an impressive place — a veritable palace of a building compared with most other places in the territory. He curled his lips into a thin, tight grimace. Obviously

Heller had not forgotten that he had belonged to the South in the old days. The ranch still held a certain old colonial look about it, very reminiscent of the large plantations to the east. There was no smoke coming from any of the chimneys, but on a blistering hot day such as this, no one would have lit a fire. A dozen or so horses were in the fenced corral to one side of the house and he could see a handful of men exercising them, breaking in some of the more skittish colts.

He sat tall in the saddle for several moments looking down upon the place where his bitterest enemy lived. The urge to ride down there, to hunt him out and shoot him down like the rat he was, regardless of the outcome, was almost more than he could control. Only with a supreme effort of will did he force the thought out of his mind. There was a lot more he had to do first. Killing Heller would ease the gnawing ache in the pit of his stomach, but it would not help these homesteaders who, whether or not they were aware of it, depended upon him to help them. He wheeled the sorrel sharply off the trail and rode back towards the river. The more he saw of this place, the more puzzled he became. A vast spread, comprising the most lush terrain in the whole territory, and not a single sign that any beef had been raised on it.

He forded the wide river which, at this point, seemed to be the boundary of Heller's spread. On the opposite bank, the nature of the ground seemed to change abruptly. The trail, when he picked it up again, dropped down sharply into the broken flats and angled sharply to the right to skirt a shielded stretch of red sandstone where a deep canyon ran alongside the trail. There were a few stunted bushes here and patches of dry, parched-looking grass which would afford little succour to hungry animals. Time after time, he turned in the saddle to peer behind him, looking swiftly over his shoulder as if expecting to see the dust raised by a group of men riding after him, coming hard to catch him up or even to run him down. Deliberately, he searched the dust shrouded country which lay on all sides of him, batting his eyes against the fiercesome glare of the sun which seemed to strike the red sandstone and shock up at him in rippling, sickening waves. But when trouble finally came, it came suddenly and from a totally unexpected quarter. The trail led between tall, rearing pillars of rock, lofty pinnacles of eroded sandstone that had been twisted by the wind into strange shapes. Here, on the narrow canyon floor, it was dark and although the air hung hot and unmoving, there was a little comfort to be had away from the direct brightness of the midday sun. His eyes fought to adjust themselves to the dimness and his limbs were cramped and painful as he tried to ease his body into an easier position in the saddle.

As the sorrel picked its way sure-footedly over the loose boulders on the floor of the canyon, where the narrow trail threaded its way between the rising walls of rock, he heard the sound of hoofbeats to his right. Instantly, he realised that they were closer than they should have been if the rider had been following him from Heller's spread. It would have been impossible for him to have worked his way that close without having been spotted some time before. Clem reined his horse for a moment and sat quite still, searching with eyes and ears in an attempt to pick out the position of the rider, batting his eyes against the vagrant dust-flurries which swirled briefly around him. Nothing seemed to move and he edged the sorrel forward a hundred yards or so, aware that it was possible in this heat, for hearing to be the most deceptive of senses and that sound travelled long distances in the silence of the buttes country. It was just possible that the rider, whoever he was, might be more than a couple of mile distant, than less than a few hundred yards as he sounded.

He ran his gaze swiftly over the red, wind-eroded canyon wall, probing every detail of it, the stunted brush which covered most of it near the top. Then he saw what he wanted, the narrow winding trail which led up the left hand face, almost precipitous in places, but still, he judged, capable of being climbed by the sorrel. Jerking his mount's head around, he pulled the brave horse off the canyon trail and headed it in the direction of the steep slope.

You invited trouble when you rode out of Senica in this direction, he told himself fiercely, *well, perhaps this is it coming up fast.*

He dug in his heels, working the sorrel upwards. There were a few occasions when he felt it slip on the rocky, treacherous surface as it fought its way fiercely up the slope towards the face of the canyon where it seemed to rise sheer above them, looming up to the blue-whiteness of the midday sky. He halted the horse in a cleft in the rocks when it had climbed as far as it was possible to go. Here, he was sheltered by the high boulders from the trail below and could also watch anyone moving along the top of the buttes if there happened to be a trail there. Now there was nothing for him to do but wait for the unseen rider to show himself. Dismounting, he sat with his back against the warm wall of sandstone where he could look out at the boulders and see the tops of the brush down below. Easing out the long-barrelled Colts, he took a look at the loads, then replaced them, satisfied.

A short while later, he spotted the rider, edging his way downward into the floor of the canyon. A moment lapsed and the man went into the black shadow and he could hear the muffled thunder of his horse's hooves on the rocky floor. He did not recognise the man from that distance, although there did seem to be something oddly familiar about him. While his every nerve screamed action at him, he sat quite still, aware that caution and patience usually played long odds in a game of hide-and-seek like this. Slowly and deliberately he slid the guns from their leather holster and balanced them carefully in his hands, waiting quietly, scarcely breathing as the man below suddenly reined his horse at the point where Clem had left the trail. He saw the other raise his head and stare upward into the blinding glare of sunlight refracted from the red rock. The other had been following him deliberately then, he told himself. There was no longer any doubt about that in his mind. Gently, he gloved back the hammer of the twin Colts. Raising his voice so as to be clearly heard by the other, he called: 'All right, that's far enough.'

There was a pause, then the man in the saddle looked up and with a little shock of surprise, as the sunlight fell full on the man's face, Clem recognised the tall, slender figure of Gomez, the half-breed.

He saw the other's right hand move down for the gun in his belt, with the speed of a striking rattler. Without pausing, Clem loosed off a couple of shots, saw the other's horse suddenly shy away from the trail as the bullets hammered against the rocks near its feet and ricocheted off into the darkness of the valley floor. Swiftly, Gomez threw himself out of the saddle and went down out of sight behind the rocks. The outlaw's gun spoke again, but this time Clem Vance was in motion. The bullet ripped harmlessly through the air where he had been a few seconds before when the gunman had squeezed the trigger. Swiftly, his glance swept about him and the corded muscles of his body suddenly constricted into a steel-like hardness beneath the brown skin. The sorrel, standing back a little way from the narrow tail had its head up, ears pricked, alert, but quiet. Then, out of the corner of his eye, Clem saw the movement among the rocks just to his right and a little distance above him. The bullet which smashed into the sandstone a split second later was less than an inch from his head as he flung himself sideways. Only his trained reflexes had saved him at that moment. He cursed himself for not having realised the possibility that there might have been two men on his trail. Lead ripped and tore among the rocks as he crouched down, keeping his head low. His position had suddenly become very precarious with the appearance of this second man above him. It meant that the other could pick his target whenever he raised his head to throw a shot at Gomez. He set his jaw tightly, and crouched down, raising his head cautiously an inch at a time. The split in the boulder hindered fast sighting but he triggered another couple of shots at the gunman among the rocks, heard a sudden scream of pain and saw him duck backward out of sight as one of the bullets found its mark.

Swiftly, he turned his attention to

Gomez. The half-breed had taken advantage of the past few moments to clamber swiftly forward over the rocks and now he was crouched down among the boulders less than twenty yards away from Clem's hiding place. Lead wailed a deadly dirge through the rocks and scanty brush. Clem snapped a swift shot in the half-breed's direction, as his head popped up for a second from behind the rocks. He saw the other suddenly jerk sideways and drop his gun as he reeled back. Savagely, Clem fired again until there was the click of the hammer on a empty chamber. As he paused to reload, Gomez staggered to his feet from behind the rocks and fled headlong down the narrow trail. He did not stop until he had reached his horse at the bottom of the canyon wall. Clem fired another shot after him, but the distance was too great for an accurate, killing shot and even as he watched, eyes narrowed, he saw the other pull himself awkwardly into the saddle and urge his mount forward, hanging low over the horse's neck. Clem felt a wave of satisfaction course through him. The other had obviously been badly hurt by that last shot which seemed to have creased his temple, glancing off the bone. He doubted if the other would stop until he reached Senica. But in the meantime, there was still that other gunman to take care of, hidden somewhere among the rocks. Throwing caution to the winds, he suddenly pushed himself to his feet and advanced over the boulders toward the spot where he had last seen the man fall back out of sight. Holding himself stiffly erect, he intentionally delayed his approach, moving from one side to the other. His sudden appearance must have unnerved the gunman completely for although two shots were fired at him, both went wide as the man missed shots which ought to have been easy from that distance. Fifteen yards from the other's hiding place, eddies of red dust whirled off the sandstone as Clem's bullets smashed around the other's place of concealment. But the man was getting desperate now. His lead ripped and screamed past Clem's head and still he advanced towards the other, seemingly invulnerable, slamming death in front of him from both sides.

Suddenly, the other rolled out into the open, his face screwed up into a grimace of fear and pain. The heavy Colts bucked and jumped against Clem's wrists and he saw dust flicker briefly on the other's shirt as the slugs hit home. His strength seemed to ebb suddenly and he fell back onto the rocks, legs sprawled out in front of him, the guns falling from his nerveless fingers, hitting the rocks metalically and bounding off down the canyon wall. Clem strode forward purposefully and stood spread-legged in front of the other, staring down at him, eyes bleak, his Colts still trained on the man's heaving chest.

Blood stained the front of the man's shirt and it was obvious that only sheer willpower was keeping him alive. A weird, bleating sound escaped from the other's throat as Clem bent over him, pulling the other's head round slowly so that he was staring down into his eyes.

'You taking orders from Heller or Gomez?' he asked tightly. 'Who sent you out with Gomez to kill me?'

The bushwhacker's eyes flicked open, fixed on him with a look of hatred. The bloodless lips drew back in a thin snarl of defiance. 'I don't know what you're talking about,' he muttered haltingly. 'First thing I know, you start shooting at me while I'm up there in the rocks. I only shoot in self-defence.'

'You're a goddarned liar,' Clem bit out. 'Funny you come riding up at the same time as Gomez trying to trap me here in the rocks. I heard you hightailing it after me some time ago.'

'Then you answer your questions.' The hatred was still there in the other's eyes but already they were beginning to glaze over, staring up at the sun.

'What about Mark Heller? You

working for him?'

'Heller? Don't know the name,' muttered the other. For a moment, the eyes held a faint gleam of cunning. 'I just meet up with this hombre who calls himself Gomez. Takes me to have a talk with the Sheriff in Senica. He reckons there's an outlaw heading for the range to the north and that there's a reward out for us if we bring him in, dead or alive. Gomez pointed you out to me. When it comes to killing renegades, I don't ask no questions, I just — ' His voice broke off and his head fell back against the rocks, his eyes sightless as they stared up at the red buttes.

Slowly, Clem got to his feet, thrusting the Colt into his holster with a sudden, savage movement. He felt sure that the other had been lying when he had denied all knowledge of Mark Heller. Gomez was merely a paid killer, one of the other's hired assassins. The real orders had not come from him. He looked down at the killer for a long moment, speculating, then screwed up his lips into a grimace of disappointment. If only the other had lived long enough to answer some more of his questions, he would have felt a lot easier in his mind. This was dirty business that he seemed to have headed into and he would need all of his wits about him if he was to come through it with a whole skin.

Slowly, easily, he swung up into the saddle. The sorrel had stood patiently waiting for him against the sheer wall of the canyon. As he rode slowly along the narrow trail and then out into the wastelands, he tried to think things out in his mind. There were a lot of things about this whole affair which, at the moment, didn't seem to tie up. They were still bothering him as he reached the point where the trail forked, one part heading towards Senica, the other down to the south, where it ran for hundreds of miles towards the distant Rio Grande.

He paused, undecided. Then, pulling hard on the reins, he turned the sorrel in the direction of town and it was at that moment that the small band of men, guns in their hands, rode around one of the buttes and thundered towards him. Flight was out of the question. It would be impossible for the sorrel, tired after that hard ride up the sheer face of the canyon, to outrun these fresher horses. It was equally futile to attempt to shoot it out with these men. They had the drop on him and even from that distance, they could easily shoot him in the back if he turned and tried to head back into the comparative safety of the canyon.

The riders, hard-faced, swung across his path. Two of them rode up behind him, cutting off all hope of retreat. Their guns covered him unwaveringly.

'Just what is this?' he asked easily, forcing evenness into his tone. 'A hold-up? If it is, you'll get little from me.'

'Keep quiet and come with us,' snapped the leader of the men, a short, thin-featured man, his hat pulled well down over his eyes to shield him from the stunning glare of the sun. 'There are some questions Heller wants to ask you.'

'Heller?' Clem deliberately puckered his brow in bewilderment. 'Who's he?'

'He owns this land that you're trespassing on,' snapped the other tightly. 'Ben — git his guns.'

One of the riders urged his mount forward alongside Clem's, reached over, careful not to place himself in the line of fire of any of the other men, and pulled Clem's guns from their holsters, stuffing them into his own belt.

'Good. Now ride, and no tricks. Heller asked that you should be brought in alive, but he didn't say how much alive you had to be. A bullet in your leg won't make much difference to him so long as you're able to talk.'

Tight-faced, Clem rode between the men as they hit the trail leading north, back in the direction from which he had just ridden. So far, none of these men had mentioned him by name, although from their tone, they had implied that Heller knew who he was, and possibly why he was there. On the other hand, the cattle boss might simply be curious about him, might merely want to know just how much of a danger he was. They cut across the river at a different point to where he had forded it and rode through the lush cattle country towards the Heller ranch. The men riding beside him were silent all the way and any attempt he made to get them to talk met with a warning glance and he finally gave it up.

Past the corral, they rode into the wide courtyard which fronted the ranch, the sound of the horses' hooves clattering on the smooth stone. Reining his mount, Clem remained in the saddle as the others dismounted. Then the leader came forward and motioned him down.

'All right, mister, inside the house,' he said harshly. He prodded Clem forward with the barrel of his gun.

There was no point in attempting to

resist. Clem walked through the porch and into the house, surprised to find that even though the sun was hot outside, here it was cool.

The man led him along a short corridor to the room at the end, knocked loudly on the glass-panelled door and waited. A moment later, a man's voice shouted something from inside the room and Clem's captor pushed him inside. He caught his balance, stood there, blinking his eyes in the strong sunlight that streamed in through the open window. Mark Heller certainly had done himself well since he had ridden out of Carson City in a cloud of dust after shooting a man in the back.

Then he lifted his head and stared across the room at the man he intended to kill. There was no recognition in Heller's eyes as he looked back at him, seated behind the polished desk by the window. But that wasn't surprising. If Heller had seen him at all on that fateful day, several years before, it could only have been a fragmentary glimpse as he had run out of the livery stables on hearing the sound of shots. But for him, recognition was immediate although he kept the look of hate in his eyes veiled from the other. So long as the man did not recognise him, or the deadliness of his purpose, he might be safe.

The man who had brought him there walked back a couple of paces and stood, leaning against the door, arms folded, watching Clem with a hint of sardonic amusement in his eyes, like that of a man about to tread on a rattler, thought Clem watching him out of the corner of his vision. Then he turned his attention back to Heller.

The other leaned back in his chair, lips curled slightly. 'I hear that you've been trespassing on my land,' he said quietly. 'Also that you've been teaming up with those nesters who've ridden into Senica.'

'How was I to know this was your land?' asked Clem, shrugging. 'The first

I knew was when these men of yours jumped me in the desert.'

'So? And what of Gomez? Do you deny that you shot him and another of my men?'

'So they were your men who tried to bushwhack me.' Clem forced the right amount of surprise into his voice. 'All I knew was that they followed me into the canyon and tried to kill me. I merely shot at them in self-defence.'

'I see.' The other's lips tightened. 'You know, seems to me I've seen your face somewhere before, but I can't quite place it; and it wasn't in Senica.' He gave a quick nod. 'You ever been back east during the War?'

'Nope. Should I?' He gasped in sudden agony as the barrel of a Colt was jammed sharply into the small of his back.

'Better answer Mister Heller's questions a little more politely,' snarled the gunman at his back. 'He don't like anyone talking like that to him.'

Savagely, Clem bit his teeth hard

together to prevent himself from crying out aloud as the other ground the gun deeper into his body. Heller was smiling quietly now. He said slowly: 'All right, that'll do. I think he's learned his lesson.'

The other man withdrew to his post near the door. Heller placed the tips of his fingers together. 'You're a very foolish man, throwing in your lot with those homesteaders, knowing that I don't intend to have them around. Don't attempt to waste your breath and my time denying that you were with them. The Sheriff and Jason have both reported to me and it's just possible that, whoever you are, you know a little too much for your own good.'

'Now listen, Mister Heller,' protested Clem. 'I don't know what all this is about. I just rode into Senica a couple of days ago. I'll admit that I spoke with those homesteaders when they were arguing with your lawyer, but all I told them was to be careful what they did, that it wasn't worth while going against a powerful organization that could kill them quite easily. If they had any cause for complaint, then they ought to see the Sheriff or the circuit judge when he come around to Senica.'

'In other words you aren't looking for trouble. Is that it?'

'I don't want to get myself killed, if that's what you mean. I'm not a fighting man. I came here looking for a job.'

Heller's brows were lifted a fraction of an inch. 'So you claim that you're no fighting man. Seems to me that you can handle those guns of yours pretty well if you could outshoot Gomez. He's one of the fastest guns in the territory. I think that you're lying. But for a peaceful man, perhaps you deserve something peaceful.' He threw a swift glance at the man standing by the door.

'Tell Horner to come here, pronto.'

'Sure, boss.' The door behind Clem opened and he heard the footsteps of the gunman fading along the corridor.

'Just what do you intend to do,' asked

Clem tightly. He allowed his gaze to travel around the room, taking in everything. Fortunately, the gunman had been too confident when they had taken him out there in the desert. They had cleaned him of his guns but had not bothered to take their search a step further and consequently, the long-bladed hunting knife was still strapped to his left wrist, ready for instant use. He half-smiled to himself as it came to him how easily it would be to kill the man sitting at his ease in front of him. But this was neither the time nor the place for that. At any moment that gunman might be back and although he could kill this man, he would stand no chance against the others until he had his guns.

'I hate trouble,' murmured the other, leaning back. He ran his gaze over Clem and there was still the faintly puzzled look in the cold, bleak eyes. He was still trying to recall where he had seen Clem before. If he once remembered that incident in Carson City then

76

it would come to a showdown. 'I'll get Horner to take care of things for me. He's a good man and I think he knows what will happen if anything goes wrong.'

There was a movement behind Clem. 'You sent for me, boss?'

Heller nodded, almost pleasantly. 'We have a visitor,' he said casually. 'He's been caught trespassing on the range. I think he knows a little too much, evidently he was snooping around for some purpose.'

'Think he might be a United States Marshal, boss?' asked Horner, throwing Clem a penetrating glance. His right hand hovered above the gun at his belt.

'That thought had occurred to me,' admitted the other, rising slowly to his feet and standing with his back to them, staring out of the window. 'If he is, I'm sure that you can take care of things for me. You know exactly what to do. He's a peaceful man according to his own words, it's only fitting that he should go out in a peaceful way.'

Horner laughed hoarsely. There was an ugly look on his face as he turned and glanced at Clem. 'I'll see to it that nothing goes wrong. When do you want me to take care of him, boss?'

'There's no time like the present. Those nesters back there in Senica seem determined to make trouble and if any of them take it into their heads to go back to Dodge and file their claim in the court there, we might not stand much of a chance. When they do that, it could have the effect of bringing the Rangers down on our necks.'

'Then mebbe we ought to take care of them at the same time, boss. I could get most of the boys rounded up by nightfall and ride into Senica.'

'Perhaps that might not be a bad idea after all. Once you've done this little job for me, get the rest of the men ready. We'll ride into Senica tonight and finish these nesters for good. Ellison reckons they're expecting more to ride into Senica within the next few weeks. If we wait until then, we may find more trouble on our hands than we can handle. Better take them in small lots to be on the safe side.'

Clem drew in his breath sharply. Forewarned was forearmed, but it meant he had to get back into town within the next few hours and warn these people, if necessary help them to meet this new menace; and that was not going to be easy. He gritted his teeth as Horner caught him tightly by the arm and swung him round, the other's fingers biting into his flesh with a steel-like strength through the cloth of his shirt.

'You won't get away with murder like this, Heller,' he snapped harshly. 'You may believe that you're the law around here but pretty soon that position is going to be altered and you'll find yourself swinging at the end of a rope.'

'Take him away,' said Heller casually. He gave a negligent wave of his hand. 'Be sure that you take him well away from the ranch before you get rid of him.'

'Sure, boss.' Horner thrust Clem through the door and along the corridor, out into the courtyard. The horses were still standing there with a couple of men seated on the wooden fence around the corral keeping an eye on them.

'All right, fella. Git on your horse and ride out slowly,' ordered Horner. He swung himself up into the saddle of the other horse. 'And if you've any ideas of trying to make a break for it, forget 'em. I'll shoot you in the back if I have to, though I much prefer to kill you my own way.'

Clem shrugged, climbed into the saddle, put spurs to the sorrel and rode out of the courtyard. He was aware of the eyes of the men on the corral fence watching him, boring into his back as he rode off. Horner rode beside him, sitting easily in the saddle, obviously supremely confident in his ability to carry out the task which Heller had ordered him to do. Out of the corner of his eye, Clem could see the faintly mocking smile on the other's lips and knew what kind of thoughts were running through the other's mind at that moment, as they rode between the tall trees leading up to the ridge overlooking the ranch-house. Without any guns, Clem was clearly helpless and the other would pick his time and place for the murder. Clem felt certain that this was one of the men who had ridden with Heller on that day back in Carson City when they had gunned down Sheriff Peterson. The thought made it a little easier to look ahead to the time when he would have to kill the other. He sat tall in the saddle now, content to bide his time and wait for the other to make the first move.

Quietly, he said: 'Just what do you aim to get out of this killing, Horner?'

'Keep your mouth shut,' snarled the other viciously. 'You're due to die and nothing you can say is going to change that.'

'You know, I reckon you're scared of

Heller. The way you and the others jump whenever he gives an order. He seems to be the big man around these parts. He gives the orders and you obey them. Don't you ever think of doing things for yourselves?'

'Keep on talking if you want to then,' muttered the other unpleasantly. 'If it takes your mind off dying. I don't want it said that I stopped a hombre from talking just before I killed him.'

'What happens to me ain't important,' said Clem tightly. 'I'm just one man. But whatever Heller thinks, those nesters are going to be a pretty big problem. I know how they're feeling right now and some of you men are going to git yourselves shot when you ride against them in Senica. I guess Heller won't be there to risk his precious hide.'

'He pays us well,' muttered Horner thickly. He tapped the Colt at his waist. 'If those homesteaders try to make a fight of it, all the better. We'll be ready for them when we ride into town tonight. They'll never know what hit them.'

'And of course, Sheriff Ellison is in Heller's pay, so the sodbusters can expect no help from the law. Just how long do you reckon the decent citizens of Senica are going to stand for you outlaws running the place? Pretty soon, they may decide to take the law into their own hands, and then you and Heller will be finished, because you won't be able to stand up to them.'

'Mebbe so, but you ain't going to be around to see that day, if it ever comes.'

The other lapsed into silence and Clem stared about him. They had ridden across the boundary wire at this point and were just heading out into more open country, where the lush grass had given place to sparsely scattered sage and mesquite. The river he had forded earlier lay some three miles to the west and almost directly ahead of them was the narrow shadow of a steep-sided canyon with stunted trees growing on top of it. Down below, he noticed that the trees themselves were thicker than elsewhere and a man's body could be lost down there until his bones had been picked clean by the buzzards and bleached white by the strong sun.

He had the conviction that this was where the other intended to kill him and in spite of the tight control he had on himself, his fingers gripped the reins convulsively until the knuckles stood out white under the flesh and he felt the muscles of his jaws lump a little under the skin. The knife rested against his wrist and he knew that it would take only a fraction of a second to flick it out and into the outlaw's chest. Then he would have to hide the body in those trees and head back to town as fast as the sorrel would take him. In Heller's present mood, he would not pause to wait for Horner to show up before sending his men into Senica after the nesters. If Horner wanted to stay out on the range and miss all of the fun that was his own look out. There would be plenty of other gunslingers around on the ranch to handle the handful of men with the wagons.

While every nerve and impulse screamed at him for action, he forced himself into calmness as the other headed his horse in the direction of the narrow canyon cut by long ages of wind and sun out of the smooth face of the desert. Down there, among the shadows of the trees, where the sunlight never seemed to reach, was the perfect spot for a cold-blooded killing such as Horner had planned. The outlaw deliberately slowed his mount as they drew close to the spot and Clem caught him glancing round at him out of the corner of his vision several times as they approached. He wondered when the other intended to make his play and tensed himself slightly, hands almost together on the pommel of the saddle, the fingers of his right hand within an inch of his left wrist.

'All right,' rasped the other suddenly, 'this is as far as we go.'

Clem glanced about him in pretended surprise. He reined the sorrel to a halt. 'So you really intend to kill me,' he said harshly.

'You heard the orders Heller gave.' The other was smiling broadly now as his right hand reached down for the gun in its holster, fingers closing around the butt. 'This ain't the first time I've killed a man like this. There were a couple of lawmen in town, elected by the people, who wouldn't take orders from Heller, even though they were warned what might happen. It was too bad they didn't do as they were told. They might have been alive today if they had.'

The gunslinger's smile broadened, showing the uneven teeth. 'This is where you git yours.' He withdrew the gun very slowly as if he had all the time in the world in which to make his play. His eyes were like polished agates in the sunlight, devoid of all emotion, glittering like those of a snake. Clem watched him closely. When a man had reached the pitch of readiness to kill there was always certain signs which were inescapable. Lips were thinned and drawn back over the teeth in an animal-like snarl and eyes turned colourless, hard and calculating.

'Ain't yuh going to beg for mercy like the others?' asked Horner almost in a whisper.

'I don't plead for my life with killers like you,' said Clem evenly. 'Besides, you won't kill me. Do you think I'd have ridden out here with you like this, without making some attempt to escape if I thought you had a chance of killing me? You must be a bigger fool than I figured.'

For a moment, he saw the startled look of shock in the other's face. Then the outlaw was back on balance once again. He began to raise the barrel of the gun, to line it up on Clem's chest, his finger bar-straight and hard on the trigger and in that moment, Clem moved. His hand shifted in a blur of speed which took the other completely by surprise. The knife flashed silver and blue in the air as it pitched, arrow-straight for Horner's chest. For a moment, he sat upright in the saddle, the gun still in his hand. Then his finger squeezed the trigger in a convulsive movement, the bullet ploughing into the sand a couple of feet in front of his mount. The look of cunning and diabolical pleasure on his face swiftly gave way to one of stupefied amazement. The forty-five slid slowly from his hand and hit the sand with a dull thud. For a further moment, he sat there, looking down at the knife hilt in his chest and the red stain that was spreading slowly around it, soaking into his blue shirt. Then, almost as if an invisible fist had hit him hard and suddenly in the small of the back he pitched forward out of the saddle and slid disjointedly to the ground. The horse shied away for a moment, hooves thudding close to the dead outlaw's head, then steadied. Slipping from the saddle, Clem went over and retrieved his knife, wiping it on the other's shirt before sliding it back out of sight in a small strap close to his left wrist. Bending, he took the other's guns, checked them, then pouched them in his own holsters. Pausing only for a moment, he hooked his hands under the other's arms and dragged him over the sand to the edge of the steep canyon. With a quick heave, he pushed him over the side, stood there for a moment watching Horner's body as it plummetted down the canyon face, crashing through the branches of the trees until it hit the bottom, out of sight. Going back, he hit the other's horse smartly on the rump and set it galloping off, back to the ranch. There was no doubt that Heller would know that something had gone wrong the minute Horner's mount turned up without him, but by that time, he ought to be in Senica and have warned the nesters of the impending attack.

The sorrel soon discovered that its rider was in a hurry to get somewhere.

The great horse picked its way swiftly over the desert, through the sluggish muddy waters of the river, then through narrow canyons, threading its way between tall buttes, so narrow that, in places, it would have been virtually impossible to pass with a couple of loaded saddle-bags. Several times, Clem looked back along the dusty length of the trail, searching with his keen eyes for any sign of pursuit. It was just possible that Heller had decided to take no chances and had sent another man after them, to make sure that Horner did not bungle the job. But when, after half an hour, he saw no sign of dust in the distance behind him, he felt satisfied that he was not being followed. Heller would probably need all of the men he could spare to ride into town and take care of the homesteaders. That was something he could not afford to lose out on. If the homesteaders, few as they were, managed to beat his men in an even fight, then it might have the effect of showing the ordinary citizens of Senica that he was not all-powerful and his reign of terror could come swiftly to an end. At a steady pace, he rode over the rough, uneven ground, skirting wide chasms which dropped down suddenly into deep bowls of shadow. Among the rocks, he rode quickly, keeping his eyes on the trail. By the time he had travelled for two hours, with the sun just beginning to drop down out of the fiery heavens towards the western hills, every dusty, gritty fibre of his body had set up a mocking scream deep within him. Before him, he could just make out the stage trail into Senica and he searched the empty plain in front of him through narrowed eyes. Far away, he could just make out the cloud of dust that marked the position of the stage as it left Senica and pulled out on the long ride into Dodge. He reined the sorrel in the shadow of the hills until the stage had moved past and the dust, kicked up by the pounding hooves of the horses had dwindled into the distance. There had been two outriders accompanying the stage on that particular journey and he guessed that this time, it carried something really important, possibly gold bullion on its way east. Once it had vanished to the east, he came out of the shadow of the hills and set his mount towards Senica. He had deliberately waited until the stage had gone past, not wanting to show himself too soon. It was possible that Heller had some men on that stage and by now, everyone would know that Heller wanted him killed.

The sorrel moved quickly through the sand, kicking up little spurts of dust as it galloped towards the town. Here lay the ugly country where few springs gushed up out of the bone-dry ground to water the inhospitable terrain. Little grew here and he rode with his head lowered, so that the sun did not shine directly into his eyes. He felt gritty and sore, in need of a bath and a change of clothing, but he knew that he would not have any luxury such as that for some time yet. He realised that he might have to locate the homesteaders once he hit town. If they had already been to the Sheriff to put their case before him, hoping for some help from the law, they were bound to have been disappointed. He did not know what kind of story Ellison would give them, but he knew that the other would do nothing to see that their claims were upheld. In that case, it was possible that the nesters had ridden their wagons out of town and were camped somewhere close by. There would be little place for them to stay in Senica itself and he had little time in which to find them.

He rode into the main street of town just as the sun was touching the western horizon and the shadows were lengthening across the entire width of the street. There were several people on the boardwalks, coming out now that the cooler air of evening made things a little more pleasant after the broiling heat of midday. None of them gave a second glance and he guessed that Heller's men were still some miles away, although probably riding their mounts as fast as they dared, to carry out their mission of vengeance. He rode the whole length of the main street but saw no sign of the three wagons which had been there the previous evening. Finally, he stopped one of the men in front of the saloon.

'Those sodbusters who rode into town yesterday,' he said quickly. 'Any idea where I might find them?'

'The nesters?' The man looked at him in surprise. 'What you want with them? Heller is getting ready to run them out of the territory. If you want to stay healthy, don't get mixed up with them. There's a showdown coming soon.'

'Mebbe so. But it's important that I find them.'

'All right, it's on your own head,' muttered the other tightly. He pointed along the street to the south. 'They headed out that way about five hours ago, shortly after midday. Probably they got scared and decided to pull out while they were alive. Once Heller and his men git here, I wouldn't like to be in their shoes. He'll kill them all, women and children.'

'Thanks. I reckon I can find them.' Clem gigged his mount, rode quickly along the street and out of the town. The sorrel was tired after the long ride that day, but it responded gallantly as he urged it forward in a gallop. Time was running out fast if he was to reach these people and warn them of their danger in time. Even then, they could still be sufficiently suspicious of him and misunderstand his motives in warning them. If they didn't believe him, there would be little time in which he could convince them. But that was a bridge he would cross when he came to it. There was little sense in filling his mind with problems which slowed down his reflexes to danger point. First he had to locate them. He knew that they would not be running away as the man outside the saloon had suggested. There had been a quiet and forceful determination in the way they had spoken the previous evening which made him feel certain they were not the type of people to run away in the face of danger. They must have endured a lot of hardship and danger just to get this far and he could not see them throwing everything away just because they had been threatened by one man.

He rode quickly along the narrow trail, keeping his eyes open for the first sign of them, but he was upon them almost before he was aware of it. The first indication he had that they were there was when two men stepped into view, one on either side of the trail, their rifles levelled at him. He brought the sorrel to a standstill and sat tightly in the saddle, looking from one man to the other. One was the leader he had spoken with the previous night. The other looked at him with a hostile expression on his bearded face.

'Just why are you trying to follow us, mister?' he asked hoarsely. 'I thought I made it plain to you yesterday that we wouldn't be driven off of our rightful land by anyone, not even your boss. If he sent you after us, then turn right round and go back and tell him we'll fight him any time he likes. If you don't, then we may decide to kill you right here.'

'I think you'd better listen to what I have to say,' said Clem quietly. 'I've got nothing to do with this man, Mark Heller. In fact he tried to kill me this afternoon, but I'm not asking you to believe that. You've every right to be suspicious of me, but for your own sakes, you have to listen. There is a bunch of Heller's men not far behind me heading in this direction. They have orders to destroy you all — and believe me, they'll do it unless you're ready for them.'

'How do we know that you're telling the truth?' snapped the other tightly. 'You could have been sent on to tell us this, mebbe in the hope that we'll run like scared prairie rabbits.' He jerked the rifle round sharply. 'Git down off that horse and come with us. And if you are lying, it'll be the worse for you.'

Clem shrugged. This was going to be a mite more difficult than he had foreseen. These people had to be convinced that they were in deadly and immediate danger. He dropped out of the saddle and led the sorrel along the trail, between the two tall boulders. The men fell in one on either side of him, keeping their rifles on him, their eyes watching every little movement he made.

The wagons were drawn up in the middle of a large clearing with a ring of boulders around it. Clem saw the women and children watching curiously as he walked forward with the two men flanking him. Probably they were wondering what it was all about, he reflected soberly. Pretty soon, unless they listened to him, they would soon find out and in no uncertain manner.

'All right, mister. Speak your piece,' said the leader quietly. He lowered his own rifle, but the other man, standing beside him, was taking no chances and kept his pointed at Clem.

'Sure. I only came here to warn you. Like I said, a couple of Heller's men tried to kill me out in the desert country this morning. Then a bunch of his gunslingers jumped me on his land and took me off to meet him, to answer some of his questions. It was while I was there that I heard him making plans to attack your train tonight. They figgered you might still be in Senica, but it won't take them long to find out where you are and when they do, they'll run this place into the dirt. I found out which route you'd taken out of town easily enough and they can do the same.'

'So you came to warn us.' The other peered close at him as if trying to make up his mind as to what kind of person he really was. Finally, he nodded to himself, as if satisfied. 'Go on. Why should you risk your life to come and warn us? I figgered the whole of the state was against us.'

'It's nothing to me whether you settle on that range out there or not,' Clem declared emphatically. 'But I aim to kill Heller myself for personal reasons. No need for anybody to know just what they are. I reckon those deeds you have are more legal than those that Heller keeps locked away in the Sheriff's safe in Senica.' He nodded at the look of startled realisation which flashed over the other's face. 'Sure, I've been through that safe. Went into the Sheriff's office early this morning when most of the town was still asleep, most that is except for Sheriff Ellison and that half-breed Gomez. They turned up while I was still in there only fortunately they didn't bother to look too closely.'

The others were silent for a long moment after that. Then the second man slowly lowered his rifle until the butt rested on the ground at his feet and looked from Clem to the leader and then back again. Finally, the bearded man stuck out his hand.

'Reckon I owe you an apology, mister,' he said quietly. 'The name's Thorpe, Brad Thorpe. This is my son, Hank. You're sure those hombres are on your tail?'

'Can't be more than five or six miles behind me,' he said, nodding. 'They ought to hit us about twenty or thirty minutes from now, depending on how long they spend scouting the area. I suggest you get a couple of men to act as look-outs on the trail into Senica. That's the way they'll come.'

'Sure thing.' The other called to two of the men standing near one of the wagons, waited until they had hurried over, then gave them orders in a gruff voice. Not until they had hurried off into the rocks did Clem feel a little easier in his mind. He doubted if Heller's men would waste time trying to sneak up on them and take them by surprise. They would figure that they had only a handful of men and womenfolk to deal with and would ride straight into the attack. Perhaps once they discovered that these people meant to make a fight of it, they would retire and use caution. But the two men in the rocks ought to be able to spot them while still a mile or so back along the trail, even in the darkness.

He checked his guns, then threw a swiftly appraising glance at the wagons. 'I reckon you'd stand a better chance of defending yourself if you placed them in a circle,' he said slowly. 'No telling from which direction they may decide to attack once they find that they can't simply run you down. How many men and guns do you have?'

'A couple of dozen. The womenfolk can handle rifles too. These killers will find that we all intend to sell our lives dearly and we'll take most of them with us if we do have to die.'

Clem nodded but said nothing. He found himself wondering how many men Heller had sent to do this job and what chance he and the nesters had of beating them off.

3

Night Attack!

The next few minutes went slowly, each dragging its way into a dark eternity when every sound in the night seemed to turn itself into that of horses' hooves drumming in the distance, heading towards them out of Senica. The wagons had been driven into position and the men and women, except for the two out among the rocks, were crouched down behind them, under cover. Every rifle and gun had been brought out and Clem felt thankful that these people had brought along plenty of ammunition and powder.

As he lay behind the wheel of one of the wagons, peering into the darkness in front of him, Clem tried to think things out in his mind. This was still frontier country, the place where greedy, avaricious men would still try to make an empire out of the rich ground. For here, there could be an empire indeed — there was a wealth of minerals in the hills to the south and west of Senica, evergreen timber and lush cattle grazing country to the north where Hiller had his land. Virtually limitless miles and acres of rich, fertile soil and short succulent grass for the best beef cattle in the country. An empire which, he reflected, was well worth the souls and lives of the men who were determined to fight for it.

But past experience in many states had taught Clem that only two kinds and breeds of men ever fought for land such as this. First, there came the cattle men with their well-fed herds, their quick-tempered range-riders, most of them running half-wild, some drawn from the outlaw bands of other states, running from the law and working and killing for any man who paid well and protected them. And afterwards there came the humbler, but equally vicious and determined homesteaders such as these people, filled with the desire to own and work the land, to take it from the cattlemen by force if necessary and to hold on to it, to shape a different kind of empire out of it. Somewhere out of this clashing and incompatible combination, law and order would eventually be forced to evolve once the towns were built and became thriving, booming communities. He shook his head in the darkness and felt a slight wave of bitterness pass through him. It had to come in the end, but it was going to be a long and painful process and he did not doubt that many good — and bad — men would die before it came to pass.

His thoughts were brought to an abrupt end at a harsh shout from the darkness which lay over the rocks in the distance. He scrambled swiftly to his feet, warning the others to stay where they were and ran in the direction of the shout. He found the two men lying among the boulders and flopped down beside them.

'Out there,' muttered one of them pointing. 'I'll swear that I saw something moving up. Looked like a bunch of horsemen but they were still some distance away and I could have been wrong.'

'Somehow, I don't think you were.' Clem's quick ears had caught the faint drumming of hooves in the distance, coming up quickly along the trail. It could mean only one thing. He expected no one else to be riding out along this trail and at this time of the night. Heller's men had wasted no time and probably knew almost exactly where they were. He wondered if they knew that he had escaped and that Horner was dead.

'All right,' he said thinly. 'Back to the wagons. No sense in staying here and being picked off one at a time. Too much cover for them here among the boulders.'

Together, they ran back towards the comparative safety of the wagons and flung themselves down with the others.

'Did you spot them?' asked Thorpe quietly. There was not the slightest tremor in his voice although Clem could guess at the effort required to keep his voice steady. After all, the other had assumed the responsibility for the safety of these people, had led them through the many dangers and hardships of their journey all the way out here from the east. Clem moistened his parched lips and held his Colts slackly in his hands, ready to use them as soon as any target presented itself. There was a tightness in his chest and a bunching of the muscles in the pit of his stomach.

Suddenly, there was a movement in the crags which skirted the trail. Narrowing his eyes, he caught a glimpse of the bunch of horsemen, riding close together as they rounded a bend in the trail and suddenly swung themselves out across it, reining their mounts. The white canvas of the wagons would stand out clearly in the darkness and could be seen easily for close on a quarter of a mile.

'Hold your fire until I give the word,' he murmured hoarsely, not raising his voice, knowing it would carry to all of the others in the silence. 'I want to let them have everything once they get within distance. No sense in sending them back under cover.'

He saw the men dismount and move forward in a tight bunch. Once they had got down among the rocks, they opened fire and bullets began to slap among the wagons, whining in ricochet off the wheels and poles. Clem pulled his head low and, a moment later, saw the gunslingers ease themselves out of the boulders and come running forward firing from the hip as they ran.

'Fire!' he yelled at the top of his voice. Gun thunder echoed back from the rocks as the rifles and colts opened up. Three of Heller's men threw up their arms and staggered back a couple of paces before pitching forward onto their faces in the dust. The others went down on their stomachs and continued firing. But they had been enticed out into the open by their own impetuousness and the homesteaders' fire was beginning to take its toll again. For several moments, all seemed to be confusion. Then the others got to their feet and fled back into the rocks where they swiftly faded from sight.

'Hold your fire,' called Clem harshly. 'No point in wasting ammunition. They'll come in again pretty soon. Be ready for them. As soon as you see anything moving, shoot to kill.'

He filled the chambers of his guns. There was now an icy coldness in his brain that directed his every movement. Beside him, Thorpe's big hands lifted the heavy Winchester and peered along the sights. He gave a faint grunt. 'What they doing now, do you reckon?'

'They've realised that we've been warned and that you're ready for them,' Clem told him softly. 'Now they'll be deliberating their next move. My guess is that they'll get their horses and try to ride us down in the darkness. We've got to be ready for that move.'

'Just let them try,' rasped the other hoarsely. 'How many d'you reckon there are out there? We must've killed half a dozen.'

'Still twenty or thirty left.' Obviously, Clem thought, Heller had intended that there should be no mistake this time. He seemed to have an almost unlimited number of men on his payroll. Small wonder that he had managed to terrorise the entire territory, forcing everyone who stood in his way either to sell out to him at a ridiculously low price, or to be buried out there on Boot Hill, when he would be able to get the land he wanted for nothing.

Lead started drumming over the tops of the wagons as the men hidden among the rocks began firing again. A bullet buried itself in the wooden upright within an inch of Clem's head and he flinched automatically, pulling his head down sharply. That had been too close for comfort. He heard one of the men utter a low, coughing cry and saw him reel back as the bullet hit him. One of the women flung herself forward with a sharp cry and went down on her knees beside him, exposing herself to the murderous fire from the boulders. Swiftly, without pausing to think, Clem flung himself sideways, caught her by the arm and pulled her down.

'Unless you want to get yourself killed, Ma'am,' he said tautly, 'you'd better keep your head down.'

'But my husband. He's been hit.'

'We'll take care of him,' Clem told her tightly. He caught hold of the wounded man's shoulder and pulled him back under cover of the wagon. 'Once we get a chance I'll have him inside one of the wagons,' he promised.

He glanced up at a warning shout from Thorpe. There was a sudden, surging rush from two sides. The gunslingers had gone for their mounts as he had warned and came riding down at them out of the clinging darkness. He fired swiftly and instinctively, scarcely seeming to take aim. But five men tumbled out of their saddles as they swept around the circle of wagons, firing savagely as they wheeled their mounts. One of the horses was hit and stumbled onto its knees, throwing its rider and rolling on top of him. The man uttered a shrill scream that was drowned almost instantly in the hammer of gunfire.

Clem counted his hits slowly, doing his best to slow down the outlaw fire as they rode around the wagons. Their attempt to ride straight through the circle of wagons had ended in failure when the three leading men had been killed within as many seconds by accurate fire. The death scream of one of the outlaws reached his ears plainly even above the thundering of hooves in the sand. There was the shrieking whine of ricochets chirruping off the metal of the nearby wagon.

As he lifted himself a little to take better aim, he felt a slug burn away across his ribs and somewhere very close at hand, a child was whimpering in fear, a little lost sound that ate at his nerves. A searing flame of anger burned through him. He fired instinctively at the fleeing shadows as they moved in front of him and everything seemed suddenly to have been taken out of his hands. His limbs seemed to move without any direction from his numbed brain.

But thanks to his early warning, they had been able to choose the position of the wagons well and the gunslingers were attacking with a distinct disadvantage. More and more of them were being hit as they rode in and no matter from which direction they attempted to attack, they met a hail of murderous fire which thinned their ranks.

Then, as suddenly as they had attacked, the survivors, pitifully few in number, withdrew into the rocks and the whine of lead ceased to hum over the wagons. Clem rolled over onto his side, then pushed himself up onto his hands and knees, lifted his head cautiously and peered into the darkness. The moon was just beginning to lift itself clear of the eastern horizon and by its faint light, he was able to make out the unmoving humps of shadow which dotted the sandy strip of ground which lay between him and the rocks. There was the faint thunder of horses moving away into the distance and he sucked in a deep breath as he wiped the sweat and sand off his forehead. His body ached and there was the warm slickness of blood on his chest where the slug had nicked the skin, ploughing across his ribs. He felt it gingerly, then decided that it was merely a flesh wound and was not serious. With an effort, he got to his feet and stood looking about him. Thorpe crawled from beneath the wagon and stood beside him.

'Looks like we beat the varmints off, Clem,' he said and there was a touch of justifiable pride in his voice. 'That might teach them to think twice before they attack us again.'

'We lost some men.' Clem told him

soberly. 'Better check on the wounded. Do you have anybody with a knowledge of doctoring with the train?'

'Sure, Luke Birkett is a doctor. He was originally heading out west as far as California, but he decided to throw in his lot with us and settle here. I'll get him to take a look at the wounded.' He paused, then threw Clem a swift glance.

'Say, you look as though you've been hit yourself. You'd better let him take a look at you.'

'Sure, later. First I want to make sure that all of these critters are dead and not shamming. I don't want to wake in the night and find that half of them are still alive and determined to shoot me.'

He walked warily among the men stretched out on the smooth sand. In the brightening moonlight, he could make out some of their faces. All bore the killer stamp and he guessed that many of them had probably fought their infamous actions during the war beside Heller, when he had fought with

Quantrill's Raiders, sacking and burning towns for the sheer sadistic delight of killing and destroying. Both sides in the war had condemned these men.

'They all seem to be dead,' muttered Thorpe finally. 'At least it saves us the trouble of shooting them out of hand.'

Clem nodded. 'The others seem to have decided not to press forward with their attack. But I reckon they'll wish that they had stayed here and been killed by the time Heller gets through with them. He doesn't like failures and when they tell him that not only have they failed to destroy us, but that they've lost more than half of their number in the fighting, he'll make them wish that they had been killed here.'

'Reckon he'll send them out again?' queried the other pointedly. They had paused among the rocks and were staring down at two of the men who had been shot even before they had got clear of the boulders.

'He probably will once the rest of his men get back from the border down south. They're driving a herd of rustled cattle across the frontier. Seems he's even running a few of his own steers with them to divert suspicion from himself. The thing that's been worrying me though, is that although I spent most of the morning looking over Heller's spread, there was no evidence that he's keeping a large herd of cattle there, yet when I first rode into town, everyone seemed pretty sure that he had close on five or six thousand head of prime beef stock there.'

'It seems to be the best of land for cattle raising,' agreed the other. 'Not that we'll keep many there once we take over our land. We're farmers mostly, Clem. We work the soil and even though I don't expect you to understand, we put more back into the soil than we take out of it. The same can't be said for cattlemen like Heller.'

'He won't let you set foot on that land without a stiff fight, that's for sure and somehow, I don't think you're going to find it easy enforcing your claim in any of the courts here. What Heller's afraid of is that some of you might go east into Dodge and register them there. The Government has a little more control there and they may decide to send some of the Rangers in here to enforce the law, and I doubt whether Heller can hold out for long if that happens. Perhaps you can see now, why he was so determined to destroy you tonight.'

'For the first time since we got here I'm beginning to understand something of what we're up against. That lawyer was right when he said that this wasn't Washington and that the same laws don't apply here. Here, the man who is in possession of the land is the legal owner as far as this crooked law is concerned, and the only way you can claim your rights is by fighting for them. We're a peaceful people. All we ask is to be left alone to work the land, grow our food, raise a few cattle. Seems though, that we ain't going to be allowed to do that.'

They walked back to the wagons. The wounded had been taken inside and were being tended by Doc Birkett. He was a tall, thin-faced man of about fifty, with hair already greying a little at the temples. His piercing eyes probed Clem's for a moment as he glanced up, then he bent over the man on the bed in front of him.

'A bullet in the right shoulder,' he said softly. 'I'll have to probe for it, I'm afraid.' He seemed to be speaking more to himself than to the man on the bed, but the other nodded, took another stiff pull at the bottle of whisky in his hand and said thickly: 'Go ahead, doc, do what you have to do.'

'Just keep a tight grip on yourself, Zeb. This ain't going to be easy, but I'll make it as easy on you as I can.'

Clem saw the sweat start out on the man's forehead as the other began to probe for the slug, buried deep into the fleshy part of the shoulder. It was probably now a serious wound, looking worse than it actually was, but it was obviously damnably painful and he saw the other's teeth bite deeply into his lower lip until the blood came, dribbling down his chin. His back seemed to arch a little on the bed and the Doctor's face was tight and serious in its utter concentration as he worked. Finally, he straightened with a little sigh of satisfaction and dropped something into the basin by the side of the bed.

'That's it.' He straightened the blanket which had been thrown over the man on the bed and gave a quick nod. 'He should feel a lot better now. He's unconscious for the moment, that last probe must have been too much for him. It's better that way, he oughtn't to feel too much pain when he comes round.' The piercing blue eyes swung round to Clem. 'I'll take a look at that bullet wound you got now, young fella.' His tone brooked of no denial.

Clem seated himself resignedly in the chair in the corner of the wagon and peeled off his shirt. During the rush of excitement he had scarcely felt any pain, but now that all of the fighting was over and he had time to pause and think, the pain began to make itself known. There was a dull ache across his chest that was worse than physical agony and his shirt had stuck to his body where some of the blood had caked into the cotton.

Gently, the Doctor swabbed the wound with warm water that had been boiled over one of the fires. 'You must've been pretty lucky,' he grunted. 'Another inch the other way and that bullet would have ended up in your heart.'

Clem gave a tight grin, but said nothing. The other worked expertly, fixing him up, pulling a bandage across his chest so tightly that he had to push the other away. 'Better not fix that thing too tightly, Doc,' he said softly. 'Reckon I'll have to use my guns soon and a man can't shoot with his chest all strapped up like a mummy.'

The other shrugged, but loosened the bandages slightly. He said quietly: 'I reckon you saved the lives of everyone in this wagon train. You're mighty handy with those guns of yours.' A pause, then: 'Now that there ain't nobody else here, mind telling me what our chances are of staying alive? I know that this man Heller won't rest until he's destroyed us all. Mebbe yesterday, he'd have been content to drive us out into the desert where we'd either starve or fall foul of some of those renegade Indians prowling these parts. But not now. We've killed plenty of his men and he can't afford to let that go unavenged.'

Clem's eyes were bleak as he nodded. 'I knew you weren't easily fooled,' he grunted, as he slipped on his shirt and pulled on his jacket. He moved his arms experimentally. 'No — you're right. He won't stop until he's killed every last one of us. And it's no use in trying to get the people of Senica to help us. The Sheriff is in cahoots with him and any posse that's been sworn in, will be to come after you.

'Not only that, but Heller is expecting those men he sent off to the Mexico border with the rustled herd to return within a few days. They'll git here long before the wagons you're expecting to arrive.'

'It don't look too hopeful for us then, does it? You reckon we ought to get the wagons hitched and pull out as soon as we can, head back where we came from?'

'If I thought you'd stand a chance of getting clear of the territory before Heller strikes, I'd tell you to do that. The trouble is, he'll have every pass and trail watched as soon as those men get back and tell him what's happened. And when he finds that Horner, one of his hired killers, is missing, he'll know for sure that I'm still alive. He'll have a double reason for wanting this train wiped out.'

'I see. Mebbe we ought to tell Thorpe. He's the leader of this band. He brought us all the way out here from the east. So far, he's made all the decisions and the people trust him to do what's right.'

'He's a brave man. But you need more than mere bravery to stand up to Heller's men. They're all paid killers and they'll stop at nothing to carry out the orders that he gives.'

'That's what I was afraid of.' The other packed his instruments away in a small case, then rinsed his hands in the basin. He was studying Clem, taking in everything about him, his eyes speculative. 'You know, there's something about you that I can't really figger out. I was watching you back there when those men attacked us. The way you used your guns, almost as if you were enjoying it, relishing the fact that you were killing those men. Oh, I know they were hired assassins, paid by Heller to kill us, and that you had to do what you did otherwise we would all have been slaughtered, but it didn't seem to fit in with the impression I got of you when I first saw you in the street in Senica.'

He snapped the lock of the bag shut

and pulled on his frock coat. 'I'm a doctor, Clem. I try to save people's lives. Whereas there seems to be something inside of you that's driving you on towards killing. As if there's a restless devil in you that will give you no peace.' He took the other's arm and led him outside, down the steps of the wagon. 'I suppose you'll think I'm just an old fool, talking like this to you, but I want you to know that if there's anything wrong, any way in which I can help you, you've only got to ask and I'll do everything I can.' He glanced up at Clem out of the corner of his eye.

'The law ain't hot on your heels, is it?'

Clem shook his head, half-smiling. 'Nothing like that, Doc,' he muttered. His fingers touched the butts of his guns, as though they had moved of their own volition, and could not refrain from hovering near to the weapons. 'You're right when you say there's something driving me on.' He hesitated, then went on slowly: 'Some years ago, I was in Carson City. The best friend I ever had was Sheriff there. Then, one day, these men rode into town, shooting up the town. They robbed the bank there and when the Sheriff went to stop them, one man shot him in the back without giving him a chance to go for his guns. That man was Mark Heller. It's taken me all these years to track him down. He covered his trail well when he rode out of Carson City that day. Several times I was given false leads. People swore they had recognised him as the man who had held up a Wells Fargo stage, but always it turned out to be someone else.' His voice had taken on a terrible intensity. 'But I swore that day I would kill Mark Heller if it was the last thing I did. I still intend to keep my word. Now that I've found him, he's going to die.'

'You can't do that on your own,' said the other sombrely. 'With all those men around him, you'd never stand a chance of getting close enough to him to kill him.'

'I had my chance this afternoon when they took me back to his ranch and he started asking me questions. Fortunately, he didn't recognise me. Even if he hears my name, it will mean nothing to him.'

'Then why didn't you kill him when you had the chance?'

Clem smiled thinly. 'Don't make any mistake about my motives, Doc. I didn't spare his life because of any softness on my part. But I'm serious about what's happening out there on that range to the north. If he doesn't run a herd of beef there, then he has some other reason for not wanting you people to get your rightful share of the land. I aim to find out what that reason is before I kill him.'

'You know what it is you have to do, I suppose,' grunted the other. He glanced about him. The night was silent except for the dismal howling of a coyote in the distance and the occasional movement from one of the horses tethered to a line strung between a couple of stunted trees. 'You'll be staying here with us for the night, I reckon. Thorpe will let you have a bunk in his wagon. It might be dangerous for you to go back to town tonight. They may be out looking for you and alone, you'd stand no chance at all.'

'I'd appreciate a bunk here,' he said wearily. There was a tiredness in his body now and a dull ache still present across his chest where the slug had bitten deeply into the skin. He did not mention the fact that he anticipated a further attack from Heller's men before dawn, but that was one of the main reasons he wanted to remain with the homesteaders.

He followed the other to the wagon a few yards away. Thorpe was standing beside it, staring out moodily into the night. He glanced round as they approached, then nodded a greeting to the Doctor.

'I've told Clem here that we can let him bunk down with us for the night,' explained Birkett. 'Too dangerous for him to ride back to that hotel in town with the rest of Heller's men still on the prowl out there.'

'Of course. It's the least we can do to thank you for saving our lives,' acknowledged the other warmly. 'There's a spare bunk in the wagon.' He turned and called: 'Zoe!'

The canvas covers at the rear of the wagon were thrown back and in the moonlight, Clem saw the young woman framed in the opening.

'Yes, father?'

'Clem here will be staying with us tonight. Get the blankets out for him.'

Clem had a fragmentary vision of a beautiful face surrounded by coppery hair that glistened a little in the yellow light. Her eyes rested for a long moment on Clem, then she nodded. 'I'll have everything ready in five minutes,' she said softly. She had stared directly at Clem with no fear in her eyes and no hesitation.

'The womenfolk all sleep in the big wagon back there,' explained Thorpe, pointing with his rifle, 'we'll bed down in there.'

'Anywhere will suit me fine,' said Clem. 'After riding hard all day, a man gets kinda weary.'

Ten minutes later, he clambered up into the back of the wagon, surprised to see how large and roomy it was. The outside had a deceptive appearance. Stretching himself out on the bunk he composed himself to sleep, knowing that he would come awake instantly at any untowards sound. He slept with one of the Colts in his right hand, ready for instant action. But there were no more attacks during the night and when he woke, the sunlight was beginning to stream into the back of the wagon, as the sun lifted itself clear of the horizon. He swung his legs to the floor, pouched the Colt and moved to the back of the wagon, looking out. Most of the others were already up and about, the women carrying water from the stream, a hundred yards away, the men tending to the horses. The children seemed content to explore the rocks, unaware of the danger which still hung over them.

Dropping to the ground, Clem walked around the wagon. There was no sign of Brad Thorpe but the smell of bacon frying reached his nostrils and reminded him of how hungry he was.

'Breakfast will be ready in five minutes,' said a warm, rich voice at the back of him. He turned swiftly to find Zoe Thorpe watching him with a slightly amused expression on her face. She cocked her head to one side and looked up into his face, tantalisingly. 'I've been wanting to talk to you ever since last night,' she said quietly. 'I'd like to add my thanks to those of the others for saving our lives when those men attacked.'

'Think nothing of it,' he said self-consciously. 'Anyone would have done the same thing in the circumstances.'

She shook her head slowly and the sunlight played tricks with the copper tresses. 'Somehow, I don't think so. People seem to treat us as though we were a race set apart from everyone else. They distrust us. Sometimes, they won't even sell us food even though we have money to pay for anything we buy.'

Clem knit his brows in puzzlement. 'But why should they do that?'

'The cattlemen don't like us because we take their land and farm it. The law, whenever it isn't crooked, just tolerates us because we have a legal right to be here. But most of the time, people try to ignore us, to treat us as if we didn't exist.'

'And now that you're here you've big trouble,' he mused.

She watched him closely: 'You're worried, aren't you?'

He nodded. 'Not only about myself, but about you. I've spoken to your father and Doctor Birkett, but I doubt if even running away is going to help you now.'

'Run away.' For a moment, she paused in her work and stared at him in hurt surprise. 'We don't run away from snakes like Heller,' she murmured thinly. 'All the way here we've had to fight. Twice we had a brush with hostile Indians and once we were nearly finished in the salt desert to the south-east. But we made it through all right and we don't aim to give up now.' She lifted her head proudly and looked at him, almost with scorn. Then her features softened. 'I'm sorry if I sounded angry, I know you're only trying to help us. But we've come so far that we have to meet this threat in the only way left open to us. If the law here is so crooked that it won't do anything for us, then we'll have to fight. We showed them last night that we're ready for them. The next time they come, they'll get the same kind of treatment.'

'The next time they come, there'll be so many of them that you won't stand a chance. You'll be overwhelmed before you know it.' He spoke soberly and there was a deep conviction in his tone which made her pause. 'I'd like to stay here and give you all the help I can, but I need to find the answers to a lot of questions and then maybe I'll know how to force Heller's hand.'

'Father was saying that you had some personal grudge against this man, Heller. That you've vowed to kill him.'

He smiled bleakly, watched her as she went about her work, getting the food ready, making every move count, apparently an expert at whatever she touched. She took the bacon off the fire which had been built in the open, broke open the baked potatoes and put dabs of butter and salt into each of them. Brad Thorpe came back into camp with the rest of the men. They were all carrying rifles and he noticed the grim expression on their faces.

They squatted down around the fire, laying their rifles down beside them. Thorpe cleared his throat, as Zoe began to hand around the food. 'We searched as far as the fork into Senica but there was no sign of those polecats who jumped us last night,' he muttered.

'They must have high-tailed it back to Heller after we fought them off.'

'I didn't expect them to hang around after the hammering they got from us,' Clem agreed. 'They won't attack again until Heller has more men to send out. He may even get Sheriff Ellison to form a posse and send them after us on some trumped up charge. That way, he can get the ordinary folk of Senica to do his dirty work for him, without losing any more of his men.'

'It ain't going to be easy, shooting down men like that, men we ain't got nothing against.' Thorpe scowled angrily, staring into the fire. 'But we still got to fight for what's ours. What kind of man is that Heller that he can give all of these orders, even to the Sheriff?'

'He's one of the men who rode with Quantrill in the war,' Clem explained. 'He's a vicious killer like the rest of the men who ride for him. He must've taken plenty of gold with him when he jumped the army and headed west.

That — and what he got from the robberies he staged — have set him up as the most powerful man in the whole territory. He's the law here, no matter how it might appear on the surface.'

'Ain't there no army post hereabouts? They would be able to stop him.'

'The nearest is at Fort Apache, near on thirty miles away. Whether the Commandant would send men out here just for this, I don't know. It's doubtful. They still have a lot of the frontier to patrol and he won't have too many men to spare. Still, if you reckon you could spare a man to ride out there, you might stand a chance of getting them here in time.'

'By God, and I'll do it,' declared Thorpe savagely. 'If the Sheriff won't afford us any protection, then we'll call in the Army.'

'In the meantime, I have to ride into Senica now that the sun's up. I want to have another talk with that crooked Sheriff and then I'll have a word with the surveyors in town.'

'You reckon you'll find anything there?' asked Doc Birkett. His eyes were narrowed in speculation. 'Better watch yourself. Heller is bound to have plenty of men in Senica right now. He may not know you've joined up with us, although he's probably guessed it. But if he figgers you're out to question anyone who can give you some evidence against him, he'll make sure that you never live to use that evidence.'

'I'll be careful,' promised Clem. He drained his cup of coffee, then rose to his feet. 'Best be on my way if I'm to get there before Heller has time to destroy anything. I suggest you try to get a man through to Fort Apache. The army are the only ones who can give you any kind of protection until the rest of your men get here.'

He saddled his horse and swung himself up, his shoulders still a trifle stiff where the bandage was still strapped across his chest. He flexed his fingers a little, checking his guns. The girl came forward and there was a brand-new Winchester in her hands. 'Better take this along with you too, Clem,' she said softly, and there was a strange light at the back of her dark eyes. 'Take care of yourself, won't you? We need you back here.'

'The wagon trail — or you?' he asked softly.

He felt a little surge of warmth pass through him as he noticed the delicate flush which rose from her neck into her face and she lowered her head a little in momentary confusion, staring at the sand at her feet. Then her head lifted and she looked him straight in the eye. 'Let's say that we both need you,' she said softly, smiling.

He looked down at her for a long moment, then touched spurs to his mount and rode out of the camp. For a moment, he threw a swift glance over his shoulder, saw the girl raise her hand. Then he had passed between the tall boulders which stood on either side of the trail and the sorrel's hooves were pounding a smooth rhythm on the hard-packed sand of the trail as it twisted between groups of short, stunted trees, their leaves hanging brown and listless in the still air. There was already the promise of the heat to come and he wiped the back of his hand over his forehead. At the moment, there was only a vague plan beginning to form in his mind. Everything depended on what steps Heller had taken to ensure his position once he had learned that his attempt to destroy the nesters had failed and that he had lost more than half of the men he had sent out. He would also know by now that Clem Vance was still very much alive and as potentially dangerous as ever, having killed Horner, one of Heller's right-hand men.

Sooner or later, Heller would start to put two and two together and begin to wonder why this stranger who had only recently ridden into town should be so set on destroying his empire. Perhaps, then, he might remember little incidents in the past, and recall where he had last seen Clem's face. When that happened, it would mean the end for one man or the other.

On the way into town, he decided to call in on one of the smaller ranches which he knew had lost cattle during the past few weeks. Here he might learn something which he could use against Heller and that crooked Sheriff. Most of all, if he was to do anything, he needed concrete evidence of guilt, and he knew from past experience that whenever men came up against anyone as ruthless and as powerful as Heller, they usually kept their mouths tightly shut, even though they had been robbed and their cattle had been rustled.

He topped a low rise, and saw the small homestead laid out in front of him a hundred yards or so from the banks of the river which he had noted earlier running through Heller's spread. There was a small handful of men down in the corral near the house and they glanced up as he rode down from the hill. Two of them swung themselves over the narrow fence and walked towards him as he reined his mount. One squinted up at him and said harshly: 'We're not looking for hands here, mister. Reckon if you want a job you'd better ride on. Mebbe Heller, to the north, could use an extra man.'

Clem shook his head. 'I ain't looking fer any job,' he said casually. 'Just want to have a few words with the owner of this ranch.'

If the other man felt any surprise, he did not show it, but merely jerked his thumb in the direction of the house. 'You'll find him over there, stranger, with one of the horses.'

'Thanks.' Clem rode into the small courtyard at the front of the house, sat in the saddle as the tall, crinkly-haired man came towards him, handing the horse he had been exercising to the groom.

'Looking for me, stranger?' he asked quietly.

Clem noticed the absence of any

guns in the man's belt, then nodded. 'Heard as how you'd lost some beef a couple of nights ago,' he said, dropping from the saddle and shaking hands with the other. 'Wondered if you could help me any.'

'Depends on what you want to know.' A tight expression flitted across the man's features and he eyed Clem suspiciously. 'You a lawman?' he demanded.

'Nope. You might say that I'm just an interested citizen with an old score to settle with a certain cattleman in the territory who, I suspect, is dealing in moonlight cattle.'

'You mean Heller?' The other nodded slowly. 'We've suspected him for a long time, but there's no proof. He's lost a lot of cattle himself and although we've tried to trail that stolen herd once, we never managed to catch up with it. Those rustlers know every trail from here clear to the border.'

'That's how I had it figgered,' Clem grinned. 'I suppose you've also heard that Heller has tried to run a bunch of nesters out of the territory because they have deeds from the Government entitling them to stretches of the range to the north.'

'I did hear something about that,' admitted the other. 'But Heller has papers too and if it goes to court, according to Jason, these homesteaders won't stand a chance of getting that land.'

'I've seen those papers of Heller's. They're locked away in the Sheriff's safe in his office. They're all forged. They aren't even worth the paper they're written on. That's why he's scared, in case the circuit judge gets into Senica and these people put their claim up to him.'

'Mebbe you'd better come inside where we can talk some more,' suggested the other. 'What you've said so far is mighty interesting. If you can prove that Heller is at the back of this wide-spread rustling, we may be able to get the other ranchers who've lost cattle to join with me and put a stop to this.'

Clem followed the other into the ranch, into the parlour where the other nodded him to a chair.

Seating himself opposite, the rancher said: 'My name's Clint Warburg. I've been ranching out here for close on twenty years, long before Heller turned up in the neighbourhood. He came from somewhere to the south-east from what I've heard. Some reckon he has a pretty unsavoury reputation and that there's some things in his past that the army would like to question him about. But so far, nobody has had the courage to face up to him.'

'That doesn't surprise me in the least.' Clem leaned back in his chair. 'I know quite a lot about Mark Heller. He rode with Quantrill in the war. One of the most vicious thieves and cut-throats in the business. Even when the war was finished, he didn't stop. He wanted power and this was probably the only place where he could get it.'

'So?' The other placed the tips of his

fingers together and regarded them closely for a long moment, brow furrowed in thought. 'I gather that with information such as this, you're a wanted man as far as Heller is concerned.'

Clem's lips curled into a faint grin. 'He's tried to kill me three times since I arrived in Senica. I've little doubt that he'll try again and won't stop until either he or I are dead. I already know too much to be allowed to remain alive. But there are some things I don't know, things that don't tie up.'

'What sort of things?'

'Like what's going on at Heller's place. He's got the best spread in the whole country and yet I haven't seen hair nor hide of any beef on it. You reckon he's lost plenty of head in the past, but just to divert suspicion from him.'

'He has most of them herded into a valley six miles to the north of the ranch. A gang of men are there almost permanently to keep watch over them.

Nobody knows how many of those cattle have had their brands changed, but we have some suspicions of our own. The difficulty is getting proof.'

'You know of any reason, apart from keeping cattle there, why Heller should want that particular spread so bad?' queried Clem. 'Part of it is so barren I doubt whether anything could be grown on it, but he won't even let the settlers have that.'

The other pursed his lips. 'Nothing that I could pin on him,' he said a few moments later. 'There ain't any gold there, so it can't be that. The nearest strike that was ever made to Senica was forty miles or so to the west and those claims have been worked out long ago, before the war started.'

'So it can't be that. Yet he must have some reason for wanting to hold onto it. Sure, it means he's the biggest landowner in this part of the territory and that, alone, will give a man a sense of power. But I've a feeling it's something more than that.'

'Thinking of scouting around to find out what it might be? I might be able to get some of the other small ranchers interested in what you've told me and they might throw in their lot with you. If you're going against Heller, you'll need men at the back of you, men who can use guns. He's hired most of the gunslingers and killers in these parts and there are more joining him whenever things get a mite too hot for them back east.'

'I'd sure appreciate that kind of help when the time comes,' nodded Clem. 'But at the moment, I'm more interested in finding out as much as I can about Heller. I know he's got the Sheriff of Senica just where he wants him. How many of the gamblers and saloon owners are in with him, I'm not sure. That's something I need to know before this whole territory breaks wide open. I was on my way into Senica when I rode here. I want another talk with that Sheriff, only this time I'll be holding the gun on him and he'll talk straight. There's also a gunslinger called Gomez, a half-breed. I creased his skull with a slug yesterday, but unfortunately it didn't kill him. He'll be somewhere around thirsting for my blood.'

The rancher got to his feet, walked over to the window, staring out. He said softly, intensely: 'When I came here I intended to build up one of the largest ranches in the state. I might have done it too, if it hadn't been for Mark Heller. He bought out most of the smaller men around my spread, hemming me in on all sides. That river you see out there. If he takes it into his head, he can dam it up on his spread and not a drop of water will come onto my land. That's one of the threats he holds over my head. The other men who own the ranches along the valley are in the same position. All of them are dominated by him. He's made several offers to get us to sell out to him. So far as I know, all of the others have refused. They know what it means. A price so far below what the places are worth that they'll lose almost everything they had.' He turned and gave Clem a lop-sided grin. 'That was when the rustling all started. When we refused to sell our land to him.'

Clem nodded and rose to his feet. 'Mebbe I'll be able to make things a little easier for you,' he said quietly. 'If I can only turn up the information I want.'

4

Ace in the Hole

Senica drowsed in the shimmering heat of the midday sun as Clem rode down the main street, eyes flicking quickly from side to side, watching the men who lounged against the fronts of the buildings, their legs resting on the wooden rails at the edges of the boardwalks. One or two eyed him casually from beneath the brims of their wide hats, pulled low over their faces, but no one made a move to hinder him as he rode up to the surveyor's office at the far end of the street. He swung out of the saddle, hitched the sorrel to the rail, then moved towards the door. Out of the corner of his eye, as he hit the boardwalk, he saw a couple of the men who had been pretending to be asleep, halfway along the street, suddenly get to their feet and sidle away for several yards, before running around the corner of one of the buildings.

He knew now that he had to work fast. Word was already on its way, either to Heller, or more likely to Sheriff Ellison. Whoever it was, they would instantly make their move against him, especially when they were told where he was. If he was on the right scent, this was where he would obtain the most damning evidence against Heller and his men.

He tried the door, but it was locked. This was something he had not anticipated. He rapped loudly on the glass pane as he saw a sudden movement in the dimness inside. A man's face peered through the glass at him, then shook his head, indicating that the office was not open. There was no time to waste. Without hesitating, Clem pulled one of the guns from his belt and pointed it at the other, motioning towards the lock on the door with his free hand. For a moment, he thought that the clerk intended to duck back into the office, hoping to be out of sight before he pulled the trigger, then the other must have thought better of the move for he came forward hesitantly, and unlocked the door.

'What is this, some kind of hold-up?' he gasped. His face was ashen, his eyes wide as he stared at the gun in Clem's hand.

'Get back inside the office and close the door — lock it,' snapped Clem harshly. He waited until the other had obeyed, then pouched the gun and moved towards the desk at the far end of the room. Here, inside the office, it was cool and dim. The clerk followed him and stood looking across at him, eyes moving from Clem's face to the guns at his waist, as though judging whether or not he ought to try to get his gun from wherever he kept it hidden. He moistened his lips drily.

'This isn't a hold-up,' said Clem quietly. 'But I need some information from you and I've a feeling that the

Sheriff is going to try to stop me getting it. And even if I do get it from you, he'll do his darnedest to stop me from getting out of here alive.'

'I'm afraid that I don't understand,' faltered the other. He rubbed the back of his hand over his chin and moved around the other side of the desk. 'Just who are you and why are you here?'

'My name would mean nothing to you,' Clem told him. 'I'm not running from the law, if that's what you're scared of. The Sheriff only wants me killed because he's in cahoots with that crooked cattle boss, Mark Heller. Now, are you going to give me that information without any trouble, or do I have to start looking for it myself?'

'But everything that I have here is confidential,' gasped the other harshly. He stared about him wildly. 'It's more than my job is worth to tell you anything concerning the records that are kept here.'

Clem shook his head. 'Very likely, but now cut the talk. I want to know why

Heller was so keen to get his hands on that land there to the north that he had the documents forged and witnessed by Sheriff Ellison and Gomez, the half-breed, and why he keeps only a token herd of beef there when that range ought to run several thousand head of cattle.'

He saw the sudden cunning look at the back of the other's eyes for an instant. The expression was gone almost before he was aware that it had been there, but he had seen enough to know that he had not been mistaken. This man might be in on the deal. Even if he wasn't, he knew the answer to that particular question. Naturally, it was doubtful if he would talk. He would try to stall for as long as possible until the Sheriff and a posse arrived, knowing that if he did talk, Heller would see to it personally that he paid for it.

'That land to the north was bought by Mister Heller when he first came to Senica, four years ago,' explained the other slowly. He made no move to get any of the records from the large cabinet at the back of the desk. 'He paid for it in gold and everything was legal and above board. You'll find no evidence to show anything different as far as that is concerned.'

'You're not only stalling, but you're lying,' snapped Clem. He leaned over the desk, caught the other by the shirt, bunching it tightly in his fingers, and pulled him forward so that his face was only a few inches from the other. 'I reckon I can guess why you're trying to defend Heller. Mebbe you're not being paid by him to keep these things quiet, but you know what he'll do to you if you do give me that information. All right, so you want to try to save your own miserable skin. Just remember that I've got this gun ready to use it on you and believe me, I'll use it if you don't tell me what I want to know. And you'll be dead long before the Sheriff and his men can break in that door and kill me. It won't help you if you're lying out there in Hell's Half-Acre, will it?'

The clerk ran the tip of his tongue around his lips. His eyes were wide and frightened now and he struggled feebly in an attempt to release himself from the other's steel-like grasp.

'There ain't nothing here to answer your questions,' he gasped out. He was almost squealing like a cornered rat. 'It won't do you any good to shoot me. The Sheriff will get you if you do that and they'll string you up from the nearest tree.'

'You don't scare me one little bit with that kind of talk,' snapped Clem tightly. He flung the other from him so that the man fell in a crumpled heap at the back of the desk. Swiftly, before the man could stagger to his feet, Clem had leapt the desk and was standing menacingly beside him. 'Now — where are the keys to these files, or do I have to blow the lock off?'

When the other made no move to answer him or get to his feet, Clem pulled the Colt from its holster and blasted the lock on the files. It fell to the floor in jangled ruin and he pulled the metal drawer open. It was filled with papers, as he had guessed. Bending, he caught the clerk by the collar and hauled him to his feet, jabbing the muzzle of the gun hard into his side so that the little man screamed thinly with pain. Beads of sweat stood out on his forehead, glistening dimly in the faint light.

'Now find me any papers relating to the land that Heller reckons he owns,' he rasped. 'And no tricks mind. This gun is likely to go off if you don't find what I want in twenty seconds.' He began to count slowly. For a moment the clerk hesitated as though unsure of himself. Then, sensing that Clem meant every word he said, and that he would shoot to kill, he reached forward and began riffling through the papers in the drawer. In a few moments, he came out with a closed file which he handed to Clem without a word.

'Now get over there and keep your hands where I can see them,' Clem warned, motioning the other towards the far wall. He had the idea that there was a gun in one of the drawers of the desk and that the other would make a break for it the minute he relaxed his vigilance. He did not intend to give the other that chance. There was no doubt in his mind that this man was merely a pawn in the game that Heller was playing around here and he did not want to have to kill him unless it was absolutely necessary. He had no real quarrel with this clerk, who was probably only doing this out of fear of reprisal.

He took the papers over near the window and glanced quickly through them. For a moment, the full realisation did not sink in. Then he knew why Heller was so determined to hang onto that stretch of land, why he had put up this front of keeping cattle on it and was determined to fight the settlers rather than allow them to move in. He tightened his lips as he swung sharply on the other.

'How long has Heller known that the railroad intended to drive their line through here and that it would be running across that strip of land?' he demanded.

The other swallowed nervously and kept glancing in the direction of the street, obviously wondering how long it would be before the Sheriff showed up with some help.

'I don't know. Some years, I reckon. That's probably the reason he bought the land in the first place. He must have known that he could hold up the railroad through this territory and if he sold out to them he'd make a fortune.'

'Just as I figgered. And that's why he's been trying to get the rest of the land around his spread.'

'And now that you know, what good is it going to do you? Do you think that you'll be allowed to step through that door alive?' There was a return of confidence in the clerk's voice now. 'You're as good as dead right now. You'll never make it out of town.'

'Don't be too sure about that,' murmured Clem quietly. 'I intend to get out, never fear. But it may be that I'll need you to help me.'

'I've already helped you more than my life is worth. I don't aim to do any more for you. You took those papers at the point of a gun. That puts you right outside of the law, mister.'

'Reckon there are plenty of folk in this territory who think the law ought to be upheld by a straight-shooting Sheriff,' said Clem laconically. 'And pretty soon, when they band together, they're going to be a powerful force, one that Heller will have to reckon with. Then you'll have to look for a new master.'

'I don't know what you're talking about.' The other moved forward into the middle of the room, edging his way slowly towards the desk. Clem swung on him, the Colt sliding from its holster in a blur of speed which stopped the clerk in his tracks.

'Don't move any further towards that

gun in the desk there,' he warned. 'If you try to go for it you'll be a dead man, I promise you.'

His tone stopped the other cold in his tracks. He stood quite still in the middle of the room, watching Clem closely. In the distance, there was the sound of shouting from somewhere along the street. Footsteps sounded on the boardwalk close at hand, the steps of several men walking with an unhurried, determined tread. A moment later, someone trod the boards just outside the office and Clem caught a glimpse of a shadow falling across the glass window. A hand tried the lock of the door, rattled it for a moment, then withdrew and a second later, the Sheriff's voice called harshly from the street: 'We know you're inside there, Vance. Better come out now with your hands in the air. There's a law in this town against breaking into the surveyor's office.'

Clem smiled grimly to himself. 'Afraid that I've discovered too much,

Sheriff?' he called back. 'D'you think I don't see through your little scheme. I've got those papers relating to Heller's land right here. Reckon there are a lot of people hereabouts who would like to read them. Then they may decide that they've had enough of this rotten justice and law you're handing out in the town under Heller's orders and may decide to do things for themselves. When that happens, Ellison, you'll be lucky if they just run you out of town after tarring and feathering you.'

'I ain't going to give you any more warnings, Vance.' The Sheriff sounded a little angry and apprehensive now, thought Clem. He was no longer quite as sure of himself as he had sounded at first. Now that he knew Clem had read those important documents and had them in his possession, the realisation must have come to him that his own job and even his life hung in the balance. Without the support of Heller and his men, with only the ordinary citizens of Senica backing his play at the moment, it was possible that Clem could swing the people against him, especially if he disclosed what was in those papers and the people demanded that he should be forced to show them. Once they discovered that he had not been lying, they might decide to take the law into their own hands and the Sheriff would get short shrift from them.

But already, Ellison was trying to shift the weight of feeling onto his side. He shouted fiercely: 'You all right in there, Clements? He ain't hurt you, has he? Don't try to shoot it out with him. We understand if he's forced you to give him those vital and confidential documents which affect all those people in the town. He's a cold-blooded killer and there ain't no sense in you risking your life. Just do as he says. We'll take care of him when he tries to get out, won't we men? We know how to handle thieves and killers in Senica.'

Clem heard the answering muttering from the crowd and knew that it would be impossible for him to get them to listen to him. The minute he stepped through that door, even if he threw out his guns first and appeared with his hands over his head, someone in the crowd, either the Sheriff or one of Heller's supporters, would gun him down, offering the excuse that he had been on the point of going for a hidden gun. He thinned his lips in a tight smile and swung back to where the clerk stood in the middle of the room, watching him carefully, trying to look supremely confident.

'You heard them,' he snapped thinly. 'Better tell them that you're still unharmed. Otherwise they may try to knock down the door and I'll kill you first if they try to force their way in.'

The other gulped and shouted thinly, his voice raised a little in pitch. 'I'm all right, Sheriff. He ain't harmed me none. But he has a gun and he's still got those papers.'

'Now don't you worry, Clements. We'll take care of this. Are you listening Vance? I'm making you an offer.

Nothing could be fairer than that?'

'Go ahead, Ellison. I'm listening.' Even as he spoke, Clem's brain was whirling, seeking some way out of this place, knowing that he couldn't possibly shoot it out with all of those men out there in the street waiting for him to show himself.

'Just come out of there with your hands in the air, turn over those papers to me and I'll see that you get a fair trial when the circuit judge reaches Senica. You've been a darned fool, but we have law and order in this town and I aim to keep it that way.'

'Yeah? What guarantee have I that you won't shoot me down the minute I step through that door?'

'You've got my word on it, Vance. What more could you ask?'

'Your words mean nothing,' he called tightly. 'I know too much about your tie-in with Heller for you to let me live.'

'Now that ain't true,' protested the other. 'I just don't want to see anybody get hurt over this. I've got a duty towards the citizens of this town to protect them from gunmen like you. The jail is the place for you until a jury decides what ought to be done with you.'

Clem listened carefully. All the time the other had been speaking the feeling had been there that he had kept talking for one reason and one only, to enable someone to sneak up on the windows, while he was unprepared for it. He glanced around swiftly out of the corner of his eye, spotted the faint shadow, thrown by the strong sunlight onto the glazed window and fired instinctively. The glass shattered as the bullet hit it and there was a yelp of pain from the figure outside. The man fell away from the window, reeling sideways as the bullet took him in the shoulder.

'The next man to try that, I'll kill,' snarled Clem tightly. 'D'you hear that, Sheriff?'

'I hear you, killer,' came the answer. A sudden switch in his tone, pitching it into urgency. 'Clements. Get down behind that desk. Right now!'

In that split second, before he could stop him, the clerk had thrown himself down behind the thick mahogany desk, his fingers clawing for the drawer in which he had the gun hidden. He seemed to have momentarily lost his fear of Clem, for he lifted himself up on his knees, pulling desperately at the drawer with his right hand, fingers reaching inside. In that precise moment, the windows facing the street were shattered into a million fragments of glass as the thunder of gunfire ripped apart the quietness of early afternoon. Clem heard the vicious hum of slugs cutting through the air close to his head as he flung himself down onto the floor. Even as he fell, his hand thrust the precious papers into his shirt, and then he was wriggling forward across the room, keeping his head down. There was little chance that the men outside would rush the office, not just yet, until they were sure of where he was. No one wanted to risk getting a slug in his heart just for the glory of being the first man to get inside.

The clerk tried to bring his gun to bear on Clem, but with a swift movement, the other shot it out of his hand, saw the man reel back against the back of the desk, clutching his wrist where a red stain was already beginning to drip onto the floor.

'Don't say that I didn't warn you, hombre,' he said savagely. 'If you try to make another move like that, I'll kill you.'

The other whimpered, but remained still. His face was screwed up into a grimace of fear and agony. Swiftly, Clem worked his way to the rear of the room, occasionally snapping shots through the smashed glass of the window. He could just make out the men in the street, outlined against the vivid glare of the strong sunlight. Several were on the opposite side of the street, crouched down behind the barrels near the boardwalk. Two lay flat on their faces in the dust closer at hand, scorning cover, probably thinking that he had been hit and in no condition to shoot back. One of his slugs ploughed a deep furrow in the dust beside one of the men and Clem's lips drew back over his teeth in a snarl of savage satisfaction as he saw the other flinch and try to worm his way back under cover without exposing himself to a second shot. The portly figure of the Sheriff was just visible on the far side, near the batwing door of the saloon. He was giving orders in a harsh voice, occasionally waving men forward from somewhere out of sight.

Things were getting just a little too hot for Clem's liking. Swiftly, he threw himself forward, reached the door leading into the room at the back of the office. There would probably be men watching the rear of the building too, he reflected. The Sheriff was no fool and would guess that he might try to make a break for it that way. But Clem had no intentions of going out that way, knowing he would be shot dead before he had taken half a dozen paces. Swiftly, he slammed the door behind him, and even as he did so, he heard the clerk scrambling to his feet and running, yelling towards the windows.

As he had guessed, there was a hatch leading up into the attic over the office and without pausing in his stride, he jumped for it, caught the ledge and hooked his fingers around it. For a moment, the whole weight of his body hung on the tips of his fingers. Then with an effort that tore at the muscles of his shoulders, he pulled himself up, knocking aside the cover with his shoulder. A few seconds he was inside and the hatch was back in place. Even here he was safe only for a little while, before they discovered that he had not slipped out of the rear. Glancing about him, he saw the small window set in the slanted roof and made his way quickly towards it. The sharp, acrid stench of dust stung at the back of his nostrils, making him want to sneeze. But time was all important now and every second was precious.

Thrusting against the window, stiff with rust, he managed to push it out of its place. A rush of hot air hit his face as he thrust his head out cautiously. He could just make out the street down below. A few onlookers were visible, but he noticed with a feeling of satisfaction that most of the gunmen that the Sheriff had called out were not there. He could guess what had happened. They had run swiftly around to the rear of the building once the clerk had staggered out into the street with the news that he was trying to get away through the door at the back. Sheriff Ellison would not be content to rely on the few men he had at the back and would send almost all of his men there to take care of him.

He heard the sound of shots from the back of the office as he wriggled his body through the narrow opening. The effort tore at the bandage wrapped around his chest and he felt it come away as he scraped through the narrow opening. Then he was out on the sloping roof, peering down over the edge onto the street, ten feet or so below him. His horse stood almost directly beneath the spot where he crouched and so far, no one had thought to look up.

Sucking in a deep breath, aware of the painful ache across his chest where the effort of getting through that small space had caused the wound to start bleeding again, he poised himself for the drop, then hurled himself out into space. The sorrel whinnied and swung away for a moment as he dropped smoothly onto its back, pulling the tethering rope free with a sharp movement of his left hand.

Behind him, there was a sudden high-pitched yell and someone fired at him from the other side of the street as he put spurs to the horse and galloped off along the street. A couple of bullets hummed over his shoulder as he crouched low over his mount's neck and then he was clear of them and heading out of town.

He hit the desert trail to the south of Senica, set the horse at a full gallop. He had to get these papers to a safe place, no matter what happened; but he knew that Ellison would send that posse after him within minutes and he dare not lead them to the nesters, or to the ranchers to the east. He decided to try to lose them in the desert, relying on the faster bursts of speed of which the sorrel was capable.

Less than ten minutes later, glancing over his shoulder he saw the sign he had been looking for. The cloud of dust in the distance behind him was no bigger than a man's hand, but he knew with certainty that it masked at least a score of riders, punishing their horses to the limit in their attempt to catch up with him. He deliberately slowed the sorrel a little as he turned off the trail and into the blazing yellow expanse of the desert. Slowly, the distance between the posse and himself diminished as the others spurred their mounts.

Satisfied that he could outpace them whenever he desired, he allowed the sorrel to get its wind. The country ahead of him was wild and barren, split here and there by deep gorges while the tall buttes rose like vast burial mounds from the plain, throwing their vast shadows over the rough scrub at their feet. The cloud of red dust expanded behind him as the riders swung off the trail at almost the exact point he had left it and came after him. He heard one or two shots, but he was still out of range of their Colts and he doubted if any of them would be able to use a rifle with any accuracy while riding at that speed.

Calmly, he led them further from the trail which led across to where the nesters were camped, deeper into the desert. The sun beat down upon his head and shoulders and the sand itched intolerably where it had worked its way into the folds of his skin, mingling with the sweat on his body. When he judged that the others had come close enough for comfort, he spurred his mount, felt the muscles of the animal lengthen as it responded instantly to the slightest touch of metal against its hide. He knew that the Sheriff would be with those men and that he and the others would not stop until they had ridden him into the ground and killed him, taking the papers back to where they belonged. He could guess at the fear that was in Ellison's mind at that very moment. He was the man who would have to go and explain to Mark Heller and take the brunt of the other's inevitable anger. Clem grinned to himself. He did not envy the other his job. He could guess at what Heller did to men who failed.

Carefully, he skirted one of the tall, rising masses of eroded sandstone and headed across the flatness of desert which lay to the other side of it, cutting deeper into the wastelands, leaving his cloud of dust for the others to follow. If he recalled this part of the territory correctly from the time when he had first ridden the trail up into Senica, several days before, he ought to hit the wooded country shortly before nightfall; and there was not the slightest doubt in his mind that the others would follow him, even through the night if necessary rather than go back and report to Heller that he had the precious papers and they had allowed him to slip through their fingers once again.

Very slowly, the sun dipped towards the western horizon on his right and still those men clung to his trail like a pack of hounds. It was possible now, to make out the darker smudge on the horizon directly in front of him, where the terrain changed abruptly and he would enter the thick, timber country, climbing up into the hills. There was a singing sense of excitement inside him as he rode towards the timberline. The odds were still stacked very heavily against him. Even if he managed to throw this posse off his trail and cut back towards Senica unseen, he still had to face up to the might of Heller's men. There was no way of telling how soon he would throw another attack against the nesters. Certainly he would not wait until they were reinforced by the other wagons heading into the territory. The sun was just touching the hills to the west when he finally set the horse towards the slope which led up from the alkaline barrenness of the desert country. The animal was tired now but it had held its lead over the others and that was all that Clem had asked of it. He glanced back as he began to climb. For a moment, it was difficult to pick out the posse against the flat, featureless background. Then he spotted them, a couple of miles back, and saw that they had split their forces. One group was swinging round quickly to the west in an attempt to head him off once he hit the trees. The other was coming up fast behind him, keeping on his tail. He smiled grimly to himself.

So that was the way Ellison wanted

to play it, eh? Splitting his force in the hope of pinning him down among the trees. He hit a patch of rough grass and went diagonally across it, giving the sorrel its head. For a long while there had been only silence at his back, but now that the others fancied they had him trapped, he expected to hear the sharp bark of a Winchester and feel the solid impact of a bullet between his shoulder blades. But he reached the trees while the others were still over a mile away. He gave a sigh of relief as the horse plunged into them. His memory had not failed him. The trail was a dimly seen track in the growing darkness. Now that the sun had gone down, there would be only the short twilight before night fell in a deep purpose swoop out of the east. At a steady pace he rode over the rough ground and began to feel a little easier in his mind as he rode deeper into the trees, keeping a tight grip on the reins, guiding the sorrel around the boulders which lay strewn in places along the trail. It was not an easy trail to follow in the darkness and he knew that his pursuers would make very slow time once they hit the timberline and came in after him, and as for that force which had broken away from the others and swung around to the north, if they rode on expecting him to burst out into the open further on, they were going to be sorely disappointed. He rode on for the best part of half a mile, then stopped the horse and listened. It was just possible to pick out the steady drumming of hooves behind him as the others followed the trail through the trees. He gave a satisfied nod, then cut off the trail and plunged into the trees, the horse thrusting its way through the undergrowth which whipped around its legs, impeding its progress. Branches whipped and stung Clem on face and shoulders as he moved through them. It was impossible to make out the dark slender shapes of the branches in time to duck and avoid them and in the end, he resigned himself to their continual cutting, slashing blows. He was more than three hundred yards inside the trees when he paused, listened while the others thundered past, the voice of Sheriff Ellison clearly heard urging the rest of the men on, shouting orders at the top of his voice above the sound of hoof beats.

Clem waited until the sound of horses had faded into the distance, then cut swiftly back towards the trail, rejoining it a few minutes later. He let the sorrel walk most of the way down the slope and out into the desert, then gave it its head. He intended to put as much distance between those men and himself as possible before they discovered how they had been tricked and turned back. He doubted if they would be able to pick up his trail in the darkness and guessed they would return to Senica, rather than spending the whole of the night in a futile attempt to track him down.

By the time he came within sight of the nesters' camp, the moon had risen and gave him sufficient light to see by. He rode slowly to the spot where he had left the homesteaders, knowing that Thorpe would probably have left men on guard and after the previous attack, they would be trigger-happy men ready to shoot at anything which moved. His apprehensions proved to be completely justified. He was less than a hundred yards from the twin boulders on either side of the trail when the bark of a highpowered rifle sent him tumbling swiftly, instinctively out of the saddle. The blow of striking the ground was pure agony and a red stab of pain lanced across his chest as he forced himself into a sitting position. The sorrel shied away for a moment at the sudden shot, then steadied.

'Hold your fire,' he yelled loudly. 'It's me — Clem Vance. I'm coming in.'

'Jest keep those hands of yours where I can see 'em,' called a harsh voice.

'And no tricks mind. I've got a rifle trained on you and I'll shoot to kill next time.'

He took the slack reins of the sorrel and led it forward slowly, keeping both hands in sight, knowing that in the flooding moonlight he made an excellent target. He came up to the boulders and two men dropped down close to him, one peering intently at him. Then the men relaxed.

'Sorry I shot at you, Vance,' said Brad Thorpe. 'Thought you might be one of Heller's varmints trying to sneak up on us in the dark.' He turned to the man with him, ordered him to go back into the rocks and keep a close watch on the trail, then led Clem towards the silent wagons. No sound came from them, although it must have woken most of them, the sound of that single shot.

'Did you have any luck in town?'

'Plenty,' muttered Clem. He took the papers from the inside of his shirt. 'There's enough here to get Heller convicted of theft and forgery. Probably enough to tie him in with murder.'

'What is it?' The other leaned forward, stared curiously at the papers in Clem's hand. 'If those papers are as important as you say they are, how come those killers ain't hot on your heels this minute?'

'They would have been, only I led them out into the desert right across to the timber country about fifteen miles away to the south. Lost them there. Doubled back on my trail. I reckon they're still trying to find their way out right now, wondering how they managed to lose me. As for these papers, they show that the railroad wants to run a line through this territory, plumb through the middle of Heller's land. He knew that from the beginning before he bought up all that land to the north. That's why he won't sell, and why he keeps only a token herd of cattle, bottled up in some valley further to the north. He has to make it all look legitimate. You never know, some day, a United States Marshal might happen to come moseying out this way when the railroad start to inquire about this one man who's holding up their development.'

'And the railroad they plan to build. Does it affect the land we bought from the Government?'

'Nope. As far as I've been able to make out, they only want a small, narrow strip of land to the north of Senica. But it seems this is the only way they can go, unless they're prepared to spend several million dollars blasting a way through those mountains to the west. And it would be far simpler and cheaper to buy that strip of land from Heller and build the railroad there.'

'If they offered him a good price for the land, why the hell didn't he sell out?' mused the other.

'Could be he was holding out for a better price, probably knowing that he had the railroad company over a barrel and they would have to agree to any price he demanded. On the other hand, it's possible that for some reason he doesn't want the railroad to run through this territory.'

Thorpe lifted his head from the intent contemplation of the fire. 'Why should anyone want to stop the railroad? That's progress and no one has the right to stand in the way of progress, especially out here in the west. This is the only way these frontier towns are going to prosper.'

'Mebbe so. But with progress comes law and order and this would mean an end to the various activities that Heller has around Senica. He would no longer be able to run this place the way he wants it. Once there was any kind of law around here at all, Ellison would soon be run out of town and a straight Sheriff elected. The State governor might also take a personal interest in the territory. I've no doubt that Heller must have considered all of these points before deciding not to sell to the railroad.'

'So where do we stand?' The other prodded the fire with a long stick, sent a shower of red sparks dancing up into the still air. 'Heller is going to fight no matter what we do. And I reckon we might as well be hung for a sheep as a lamb. I've sent one of the men out to Fort Apache. If the troopers arrive in time we may get our law and order sooner than we expect. If they don't, then we're back where we started. We'll have to fight him ourselves, with the weapons we have.'

'There's just the chance that you may have some allies,' said Clem soberly.

'Allies? You mean there are some folk around here who haven't thrown in their lot with Heller and are willing to join us in fighting him?' There was a note of undisguised surprise in the older man's tone.

'I've been talking to some of the small ranch owners in these parts. They are all pretty certain that Heller is the man behind the rustling of their cattle, in spite of the fact that he claims to have lost over a thousand head himself over the past four months. But that seems to be only a front to cover up his own activities. There's nothing easier than to get his own men to drive the cattle south and then head back with those bearing his brand, driving them in by a roundabout route. It could explain why he keeps most of his cattle in that valley far to the north of his spread, away from snooping eyes.'

'And these men are willing to fight?'

'They say they are. All they wanted was information, proof that Heller has been double-crossing them. I think these papers will be sufficient to prove that to their satisfaction.'

'So you're going to show those documents to them tomorrow.'

'That's right. If everything works out the way I hope, we may be able to raise quite a powerful fighting force to meet Heller on his own ground and carry the fight to him.'

'Then you can count us in with you,' declared the other emphatically. 'We don't hold with ranchers. Usually we find that we're on opposite sides of the fence, since they try to turn us off the range, claiming that it's theirs. But in this case, we'll fight with them against Hiller.'

'Good.' Clem yawned and rubbed his tender, smarting eyes. He got to his feet a little unsteadily. 'Reckon I'll turn in now. Better get some sleep before the morning.'

'Of course.' The other stood up, grasping the rifle purposefully. 'I ought to have known that you'd been riding hard all day. Here's me talking my big mouth off all this time.' He jerked his thumb towards the wagon nearby. 'You'll find your bunk in there. I guessed you might be back.'

'Thanks.' Clem clambered into the back of the wagon, pulled off his jacket and shirt and riding boots, and stretched himself out under the blanket. In here, the air was warm but without the terrible heat of the day and, within minutes, he was asleep.

When he woke, it was sun-up and it seemed all of the camp was awake. There was the smell of chow in the air and he dressed quickly, dropped to the ground and walked around to the fire. Zoe was there, bending over the long-handled pan on the fire. She turned quickly as she felt his gaze on her and flushed a little. Then she smiled a welcome and walked towards him.

'Father said you got back in the early hours of the morning,' she said brightly. 'I expect you're hungry.'

'I could eat a horse,' he said, grinning.

'At least we haven't got to that yet,' she retorted. 'There's plenty of bacon and beans. Help yourself, before the others get here.'

He took her advice, filled his plate and squatted down beside the fire. He ate hungrily while Zoe plied him with questions. Her face assumed a hopeful expression when he told her that it was possible the ranchers and their men would join them in the fight against Heller and his killers, now that he had proof of their double-crossing. But first he had to get the papers into the hands of these men and he knew that this would not be easy. Heller would have been alerted by now and his men would be out with orders to shoot him down on sight. To go into Senica now would be courting disaster, inviting a bullet in the back from ambush.

'You think Heller will have his men watching every trail from here into Senica and through to the north, is that it, Clem?' asked the girl, her eyes sombre.

He nodded. 'If I can only get to the ranchers without being spotted by his men, I stand a good chance of talking them round to our way of thinking.'

'Be careful, Clem.' She looked at him, vaguely troubled.

He nodded, checked his guns and the cartridge belt around his waist. Several of the small leather loops were empty now but if luck remained with him, those few shells that he had would be enough. And if not, he would undoubtedly be dead so it made little difference, either way.

He laid his plate down by the fire and

lifted his head. The girl said softly: 'Have you noticed how quiet it is out there? They haven't put in an appearance all night, even though we expected them to be back and were ready for them.'

'Yeah. I suppose they're out there covering every trail.'

'How do you reckon on slipping past them?'

Clem bit his lower lip. 'I'll need to circle around to the east. No sense in taking the Senica trail. It isn't going to be easy riding through that country, but it may be the only way they ain't watching.'

'Mebbe so, but if they're as desperate to stop you as you think they are, they'll be watching all of the trails into the various ranches around here. Heller will know why you took those papers. He won't be sitting still waiting for you to make your move first.'

'Reckon that's a risk I'll have to take. Somehow, I've got to get through to them. If they once figger I'm dead, then they'll never rise up and fight Heller. They're not exactly cowards, but they're leaderless, they won't band together. Somehow they don't seem to realise that there's strength and security in numbers and that no man is bigger than the law, when the law is represented by the ordinary, decent citizens of the towns.'

'If only we could get help from the troopers. Surely they ought to be the men to establish and maintain law and order in these frontier towns.'

'Perhaps. But the trouble is that they have so few men and such a wide area to patrol they can't spare soldiers to look into every little problem, they expect the sheriff and his deputies to take care of things like this.'

'And in a case where the Sheriff is crooked and in the pay of men like Heller, what then?'

Clem shrugged. 'Then the people either take care of it themselves, or they do what we're doing, bring it to the notice of the military and hope that they will do something about it. But in the meantime, we have to take matters into our own hands, just in case we get no help from them. With every hour that passes, Heller gets stronger. We have to strike soon, and strike hard with every man we can get.'

'Clem,' she said, searching him with her eyes. 'You will take care of yourself, won't you?' She gave him a half-hopeful smile. 'I'd ride with you if you wanted me to.'

'If all of the citizens of Senica were like you, Zoe,' he said quietly, 'I'm sure that Heller would have been finished long ago. Unfortunately, it seems to be a rare thing to find anyone with a courage like yours.'

He saw Brad Thorpe and Doc Birkett before he rode out of camp. The doctor insisted that he should open his shirt so that he might take a look at his handiwork. He probed the wound gently, then nodded. 'Looks all right,' he said tightly. 'Better be careful with it though, it hasn't begun to heal properly yet. It'll be some weeks before it's completely better.'

'You did an excellent job on it, Doc,' he said, smiling. 'I won't say that I like it being strung up with this bandage, but in the circumstances, I reckon I'd better wear it.'

'If you don't you'll have to answer to me,' declared the other in mock seriousness. 'I hear that you intend to ride out and try to get through to some of the ranchers with some papers you took from the surveyor's office in Senica. I reckon I ought to warn you that I rode into Senica yesterday afternoon and things look mighty ominous to me.'

'You rode into Senica?' Clem looked at him in astonishment. 'I thought those people there had declared war on all of your homesteaders.'

'Reckon they have. But they don't seem to bother with me none. Mebbe they reckon that, as a doctor, I'm a sort of privileged person. Ain't had a bullet fired at me in anger yet — except when those hombres attacked the train a couple of nights ago. But I reckon that was something different.'

'Just what did you find in town?' asked Clem. This might be something important but he wasn't sure.

'That hombre Heller was there trying to swear in every roughneck in town as a deputy. The Sheriff had gone out of town, high-tailing it after you, I reckon. But Heller seemed to be the real authority there.'

'There doesn't seem to be any doubt about that. This is showing him in his true colours now. He's got to come out into the open and do things for himself if he's to be sure that they're carried out properly. Too many things have happened to ruin his plans so far that he can't afford to take many more chances. If he allows his reign of terror to slip just one little bit, the people will turn against him. That's all he has to hold them in check.'

'I don't expect they can really be blamed for following him in this way. I gathered from some of the townsfolk that he holds mortgages on all of their homes. If they don't do as he tells them, he simply forecloses and puts them out. They don't even get a chance to sell out to him.'

'Then the sooner we stop him, the better.' Clem hitched his gunbelt a trifle higher about his waist. 'I doubt whether his men will attack you again in full daylight. If they mean to fight, they'll wait until nightfall.'

'Don't worry, we'll be ready for those murdering coyotes whenever they decide to come again.' There was a note of conviction in the older man's voice which Clem found heartening. As he swung up into the saddle he glanced behind him in the direction of the fire and saw Zoe Thorpe watching him. For a moment as she lifted her head, he fancied he saw tears in her eyes, but he could not be sure. An instant later, he touched spurs to his mount and galloped out of the camp, heading to the east of the trail into Senica.

He hit the bad country a few minutes later. The ground underfoot was soft and white with alkali and the dust raised by the horse's hooves bit cruelly at the back of his throat. The sorrel plodded steadily onward, head down as the sun beat down into his face, almost blinding him, beating dully against his brain, even through closed lids. The sunglow in the overhead dust was sickening, beating down in endless waves against the top of his head. High up, buzzards wheeled like tattered strips of black cloth against the harsh, blue-white mirror of the sky.

5

Bushwhack Trail

Clem Vance shoved back the broad-brimmed shapeless hat onto the back of his forehead and squinted up at the sun now moving slowly towards its zenith. The white glare of the alkali flats shocked up at him from every direction. It needed another five miles before he reached the other side of the desert and he knew there would be no water-holes in that direction, and that he had been wise in filling his canteen to the brim back at the camp before setting out. For almost a couple of miles, he allowed the sorrel to take its own time. In the desert, away from water, a man does not hurry and live. He keeps the brim of his hat well down over the back of his neck, watches the wheeling specks of the black buzzards overhead, and has only the spinning dust devils for company, and all the time there is the harsh, sharp taste of alkali at the back of his throat, choking him.

The trail here was not well marked. Few men ever used it, keeping to the more northerly trail which skirted the dust flats and wended its way through more pleasant, safer country. Only a few gophers and those seeking to keep clear of the law came this way and took the risk of thirst and sunstroke in this terrible place.

He kept his eyes moving, alert for danger. It was just possible that Heller would have some of his men watching this route too, although he would have most of them posted along the northerly trail. In front of him, the narrow trail wound and twisted, following the long canyons, gradually swinging north although he estimated that it was still within sight of the main trail used by the wagons and stage coaches on their way into Senica. He rounded a low hill which rose, hump-backed from the white plain, crossed a flat plateau of land where the sun beat down upon him with an unabated fury and put the horse down into a second canyon where there was a little shade from the intolerable glare, but no diminution in the heat. The horse's hooves crunched over the sun-baked ground as Clem rode in silence, speculating. He watched the grim, sandstone peaks with a keen gaze. When a man rode into danger like this, it could be all around him, on every side, ready to strike when he least expected it. Coming out of the canyon, into the savage glare of sunlight, he touched spurs to the mount, feeling a grim, vicious excitement beginning to rise within him.

There was a singing tension in every muscle and fibre of his lean body, almost, he thought, as if he were looking forward to the showdown which would inevitably come. Then, without warning, a rifle barked, a flat and ugly sound, that shattered the clinging stillness of the desert, sent the buzzards wheeling in ever-tightening circles overhead, and jerked him abruptly out of the saddle. He heard the faint hum as the slug sang close, burning the air in front of his body as he pitched sideways, hitting the soft sand and rolling several yards towards the cover of a mesquite bush, where he lay still, playing an old Indian trick. Swift as he had been when he had thrown himself out of the saddle, his right hand had snaked for the gun at his belt and now it was cradled in his fist, beneath his body, but ready for instant use as soon as the polecats who had tried to bushwhack him showed themselves.

His eyes were narrowed to mere slits but through them he could watch the desert in the direction from which that rifle bullet had come. Whoever had fired the shot had been watching him from a distance and had been almost a quarter of a mile away, where the nearest cover lay. Scarcely daring to breathe, he lay quite still, aware that the sorrel stood a few feet away, between him and the man who had tried to kill him. For several minutes, feeling the heat of the sand touching his body with a searing finger, he lay there, not moving, playing possum. At first, nothing moved. Then, in the distance, he heard the faint sound of a horse coming nearer, the hoofbeats muffled by the sand; a moment later he saw the two men clearly as they rode forward, one holding the rifle ready over the pommel of the saddle, the other sitting upright, his hands close to the guns at his waist.

They came close enough for Clem to make out what they were saying. The taller of the two, the man with the rifle said gruffly: 'Sure I hit him? When I use a rifle I never miss. Didn't yuh see the way he fell out of the saddle?'

'Be careful,' warned the other. 'If this is Vance, he's a tricky customer. We've got to make sure he's dead before we go back to Heller.'

'We've also got to be sure it's Vance.'

'Who else would it be, trying to sneak across the flats? Nobody uses this trail now except for the rest of the boys when they head up from the border. It's Vance all right. Now that he's buzzard meat reckon we'd better search him for those papers. He could've left them with the nesters, but I don't reckon he did. Too important. He'd be riding this way to show 'em to his rancher friends. Heller has been mighty curious about the way they've been acting lately. Seems they know he's the man behind this rustling. They could be deciding to band up against us.'

'Then the sooner we finish this job, the better. There could be a nice fat bonus in it for us.'

They slid out of the saddle and then came forward, the tall man in the lead, holding his rifle pointed towards Clem. Every muscle still and unmoving, he waited until they got within twenty yards, then swiftly galvanised himself into action. He saw the flicker of awareness on the part of the man with the rifle, saw him try to bring it up and squeeze the trigger in the same instant that his own Colt roared twice, bucking against his wrist. The first man died within seconds, as the slug found its way unerringly into his heart. He toppled forward, the rifle dropping from his hands, hitting the sand a moment before his dead body fell on top of it. The second man tried to go for his own guns. His hands flashed downward with the speed of striking snakes. The guns were halfway out of their holsters when he died. Losing his hold on his guns, his hands fluttered up to his chest where the small black hole showed quite plainly in the glaring sunlight. He stood teetering for a long moment, screwing up his eyes as if trying to see what had hit him. Then he gave a loud sigh and slumped over the body of his companion.

Slowly, Clem got to his feet, pouched the gun and walked forward, turning the two bodies over with the toe of his boot. There was no doubt about it.

They were both dead. He whistled to the horse, climbed up into the saddle and wiped the perspiration from his brow with the back of his hand. Over his head, the buzzards were dropping lower in wheeling circles, sensing that the age-old drama of death had once again been played out beneath them.

He rode with tightened lips towards the far edge of the flats. Heller had lost time in getting his men out after him, he reflected. That meant he might encounter more on the trail to the ranches. Everything was now poised for the inevitable showdown, events rushing swiftly to a climax. He forced himself to think as he rode. He could expect the Sheriff to have ridden back across the mesa after discovering the trick he had played on them the previous night, and the other would be smarting under the indignity of being shown up in front of the men he had been leading.

By the time he reached the opposite edge of the alkali flats, he was drinking almost continually from his canteen, the brackish water scarcely moistening the inside of his mouth and very little of it found its way down his throat, being absorbed by the dry lump of his tongue. The sorrel too, was in little better condition, but it responded gallantly as he rode over the rough, craggy country which lay between himself and the stretching pastures of the small ranchers who occupied this stretch of territory.

Here, the country was more wooded as he approached the Warburg ranch. This was to be his first stop. The other had offered to help and it would be up to him to decide whether the papers which Clem carried inside his shirt were the real evidence they needed, and if so, he would then get in touch with the other cattlemen in the area. All in all, Clem figured that these men could muster somewhere close on a hundred men if they all decided to throw in their hands with him and ride against Heller. The forces ought to be pretty evenly matched by them, he concluded, depending upon how many men the sheriff was able to swear in to help Heller and how many men were in that rustling party now heading back from the border as fast as their mounts would carry them.

With an effort, he put the thoughts out of his mind. Although there was a plan beginning to form, it would not be wise to make any decisions until he knew how these ranchers and the men under them would act. So much depended too upon Warburg's power of persuasion. It was not likely that these small men would dare to go against Heller unless they were pretty sure they would come out on top. He was a terrible man to make into an enemy and so far their existence here had been a precarious one. The first wrong move they made could be the end of them if Heller sent his killers out with orders to burn and destroy.

He rode swiftly through the trees which boarded the Warburg spread and it was as he neared the ranch house that he heard the sound of shots in the distance. For a moment, he reined the horse and sat stock still in the saddle, trying to judge the direction from which they came and the number of gunmen. Through the trees, he could see nothing, but some hidden sense told him that the firing came from Warburg's ranch and that this might have something to do with Heller.

He gigged his horse, rode swiftly through the trees and came out into the open a quarter of a mile from the ranch. His keen-eyed gaze took in every detail in a single glance.

Heller had decided not to wait for the outcome of the Sheriff's attempt to kill him, or those of his men spread out along the various trails into this part of the territory. He had taken matters into his own hands, attacking the isolated ranches one by one, determined to wipe out any organised opposition from this source before they could band together and mass an army of fighting men.

Return fire was coming from the barricaded windows of the ranch house and a few rifles were also firing from the barn, a hundred yards to one side. Inside the corral the horses were beginning to panic as the rifle fire barked and echoed around them. Several were thrusting heavily against the wooden fence which had been built around the corral and Clem guessed at Heller's intentions instantly. None of his men were able to get sufficiently close to the corral to free the horses there for fear of being hit by the heavy and accurate fire from the house, fire which commanded every approach to the corral. So the other was deliberately ordering his men to shoot over the heads of the frightened animals, hoping by that method to stampede them into such a frenzy that they would knock down the fence and escape.

Swiftly, Clem cast about him for some means of aiding the men inside the ranch. To ride down there with guns blazing and try to break a way through the ring of guns which Heller had forged around the ranch would have been useless and suicidal. He would have to run the gauntlet, not only of Heller's men but of the fire coming from the house too. Then his gaze lit on the large wagon at the top of the gentle slope about two hundred yards to his right. A swiftly appraising glance told him that its path would take it right through the tightly bunched men at the bottom of the slope. And the hay which lay stacked high inside it would make an excellent torch.

Slipping out of the saddle, he tethered the sorrel to one of the branches, then ducked down and began to move as swiftly as possible through the tall grass on top of the hill, keeping his head low so as not to be spotted from below. The sound of gunfire reached a thunderous crescendo as he cut across the side of the hill towards the wagon. Two blocks of wood had been thrust beneath the wheels to act as a brake and prevent it from rolling down the hill. Clem gave them a swift glance, then rose to his feet behind the wagon, using it as a shield to prevent any of the men from seeing him, but they were all too interested in what was happening inside the house.

Dimly he heard a voice which he recognised instantly as belonging to Heller: 'Can you hear me in there, Warburg? This is your last chance. We don't want to kill you or destroy your ranch. I've made you a fair offer for your house and land. All you have to do is come out here and we'll talk it over like gentlemen.'

'You ain't fooling me, Heller,' roared Warburg from behind one of the windows. 'I've met your sort before. I'd be shot dead before I'd taken a couple of steps outside. You and your hired killers want to rule this territory by fear. Well, we've taken all we intend to take from you. I ain't selling out.'

'That your last word, Warburg?'

'That's my last word. And the first man who tries to set foot inside here will get himself shot.'

'Then you've asked for it.' There was a harsh anger in Heller's voice now. He yelled something fiercely to his men and a fusillade of shots crashed against the windows of the ranch. Clem waited no longer. Swiftly, he struck a sulphur match and held it against the straw and hay. Dried by long weeks in the scorching sun, it caught easily and within moments, it was ablaze. Knowing that it would be seen now within seconds, he bent and knocked away the restraining blocks of wood beneath the front wheels. Slowly, the wagon began to move, gathering speed as it went down the slope, bouncing and swaying a little from side to side. There was scarcely any smoke. The flames boiled up from it as it plunged headlong over the stones and grass, heading straight for the bunched outlaws at the bottom of the slope. One man, acting on some strange instinct, turned his head for an instant and saw it hurtling towards them. Clem saw him open his mouth to yell a warning, but it was too late. In that instant, it crashed through them, hurling sparks and blazing straw in all directions. Two men were crushed beneath the wheels. The others tried to get to their feet and flee. Taking his life in his hands, Clem leapt down the slope, both guns out and blazing an arc of death as he reached the bottom and began firing swiftly and accurately at the fleeing men who had turned to run. Crouching down beside the fence of the corral, he dropped two men before they could reach their horses. A bullet struck the ground close to his leg and chirruped into the distance. Now Heller's men were totally demoralised by this new turn of events. They scattered in little frightened groups as the men inside the ranch continued to pump slugs into their running bodies. Clem fired off another couple of shots, tried to spot Heller among the men, but there was no sign of the cattle-boss. Then he spotted the other. Heller had not waited to see the outcome of the battle. Thinking only of his own skin, he had taken to his horse and was now disappearing over the hill to the west. It was too late to go after him now, thought Clem bitterly as he turned and ran towards the house. The other had too good a lead and might know where more of his men were hiding out, leading Clem directly into an ambush.

He reached the door of the ranch. It opened as he came up to it and Warburg stood framed for a moment in the opening. He grasped Clem's hand and pulled him inside, shutting the door swiftly behind him.

'I figgered that it might have been you up there,' he said hoarsely. 'Good job for us you turned up when you did or we might all have been killed. We were running short of ammunition when you arrived.'

'I reckon most of them are finished,' nodded Clem. He pouched his guns. 'That seemed the only thing I could do that would have had any effect on them. There must have been forty men out there. Fortunately, they were mostly bunched together at the right place at the bottom of the slope otherwise it might not have been such a good plan after all.'

There were still some guns barking at the windows, but the fire was gradually beginning to dwindle now as the outlaws tried to make good their escape. Almost half of them had been killed, either by the rifle fire or the blazing wagon which had ploughed a trail of death through them, killing half a dozen or so within as many seconds.

'Did you see Heller out there?' muttered Warburg tightly. 'I spotted him a little while ago, tried to get a shot at him, but missed.'

'He took off the minute things looked as if they were going against him,' Clem said bitterly. 'He had too good a lead for me to go after him, but I reckon we know where to find him when the final showdown comes. His reign of terror is just beginning to come to an end. I think he knows it and he'll do everything in his power to prevent it. He may be riding into town now, trying to get the Sheriff to swear in a hundred men or so to form a posse. He'll think of some charge he can trump up against you and make it stick long enough to hang you.'

'I thought he would have had enough of it after this afternoon.' The other went over to the cupboard that stood at the far side of the room and brought out a bottle and two glasses. 'You look as if you need this,' he said quietly. 'Been riding across the flats on your way here?'

'That seemed the best way to come if I wanted to miss any men Heller might have watching for me. As it was, I ran into two of them.'

'What happened to them?' The other lifted his craggy brows in an interrogatory line.

'They're lying back there right now. Plenty of buzzards around too.'

'You seem to bear a charmed life,' grinned the other, tossing back the liquor in a single gulp. 'We lost three men and two have been hit during the fighting. But I'm forgetting the reason for your mission. Did you get away with any evidence? I heard that the Sheriff was on the warpath yesterday after someone held up the surveyor's office. That couldn't have been you, I suppose.'

'Sure.' Clem nodded and brought out the papers, handing them to the other. 'Reckon that these will convince your friends of the kind of man Heller is?'

A few stray shots sounded as Warburg took the papers and read through them, scanning the pages. As he read, the expression on his face changed. Clem could see how his grip on the pages tightened. Finally, he looked up at Clem. 'I don't know how you managed to get hold of these without being killed. But I do know why it is that Heller wants you dead and will go to any lengths to achieve it. These papers are dynamite. Just what do you intend to do with them?'

'I thought you'd better keep them, show them to the other ranchers. If they can force their hand and bring them in on our side, we ought to have a sizeable force ready to ride within the next few days, a force big enough to crush Heller and any men he may have.'

The other nodded slowly. 'It isn't going to be easy. Now that he knows you have these papers and that you're here, he'll guess what's happening and he'll do all he can to stop it. Besides, when the others learn of what he tried to do today, here, it may make them pause and think again. No man wants to see his ranch and everything that he's built up for over twenty years, burned down and destroyed right in front of his eyes and that's what Heller will do if he gets his chance.'

'Don't you see, that's why we have to get together and fight him. If you ranchers remain isolated, then he'll simply take you one at a time. Together, he can't destroy you.'

'I'll talk with the others,' promised

Warburg. 'It might be better still if you were to talk to them. Take the papers with you and produce them at the meeting.'

Clem pursed his lips. There were still many things he had to do, questions he had to have answered, before he felt himself in a strong enough position to destroy Heller. He wanted to get Sheriff Ellison on his own and question him.

At last, he nodded. 'If you think that would be best, I'll do it, of course. But you'll have to hurry. When and where can you get these ranchers to meet?'

'This evening — right here,' suggested the other. 'I doubt if Heller will attack this place again.'

'He may try to attack the other ranches. He won't stop until you've all been destroyed.'

Warburg pursed his lips and pondered that for a long moment. Then he shook his head. 'He'll wait until those men reach him from the south. They'll have been on the trail for the best part of three days now. Probably they're holed up in the desert to the south, waiting for orders to move in.'

'Could be. I'll ride into town for a little talk with that crooked Sheriff. In the meantime, you get every man you can who's capable of handling a gun. I'll make it back here by nightfall, but if anything should go wrong, don't wait for me but go ahead without me.' He dug into his shirt. 'Reckon you'd better keep these papers in a safe place after all. There's just the possibility that Ellison may be expecting me. It's doubtful. The place they'd last think of looking for me is somewhere in town. But we can't afford to be careless.'

★   ★   ★

The sun was westering by the time he approached the outskirts of Senica and rode into the side street, well away from the main street where trouble could be expected. There were few people around on the streets. Probably, he guessed, most of them had been sworn in by the Sheriff and were out scouring the countryside for him. If that were the case, it suited his purpose. It meant there would be fewer men to keep an eye open for. He doubted if Ellison himself would be out there leading the posse. He would have had enough riding clear across the desert the night before and then finding nothing at the end of the trail. If he knew Ellison, the Sheriff would be seated at his ease in the office at the corner of the street two hundred yards away, leaving all the hard, dusty work to the men he had sworn in, taking his ease. He grinned tightly to himself as he dismounted and began to work his way forward between the low buildings, moving from shadow to concealing shadow. But it was a grin that held nothing of mirth in it, merely a skinning of his lips across his teeth; a grin which held something unutterably savage in it and which boded ill for Ellison.

Sweeping his eyes from side to side, he reached the place where the narrow, deserted street linked up with Senica's main thoroughfare. He kept his head well down, his face hidden beneath the wide brim of his shapeless hat, one gloved hand always hovering close to the butt of the Colt at his right side. A bullet could come from any of the windows overlooking the street. For all that he knew, Ellison might have anticipated this move on his part and there could be a hundred guns trained on him that very moment with some extremely itchy fingers curled around the triggers.

Taking a deep breath, he stepped out onto the boardwalk and made his way along the fronts of the buildings. At the first sign of hesitation, he knew, he would give himself away completely. He could only continue to walk along the street, hoping that anyone who did turn casual eyes in his direction, did not recognise him as Clem Vance, the most wanted man at that moment in the whole of the Senica territory.

He kept his eyes moving, ahead of

him, to either side and once or twice behind him as he turned his head slowly, with a seeming casualness. There was an emptiness, a curious frigidity in the town as he paused in front of the Sheriff's Office. A quick glance up and down the street was sufficient to tell him that he had not been spotted, but in spite of this, there was a warning bell ringing somewhere at the back of his mind. It was something that worried him. In the past he had learned never to disregard this. Everything looked too simple, was too quiet, for it to be anything but a trap. And yet he could see no sign of where men might be hidden waiting to jump him the minute he stepped through that closed door and into Ellison's office. He shrugged mentally. This was a chance that he would have to take. He loosened the gun at his waist, straightened up and twisted the handle of the door, jerking it open and going inside. His face felt tight and cold as he swung the door shut behind him, twisting the key in the lock. He had got this far without running into trouble, but there was no sense in failing to take the most elementary precautions.

Sheriff Ellison was seated in the swivel chair at the back of the desk. His back was to Clem as the other walked in and he did not turn immediately, but said without looking round: 'Well, any news of that goddarned Vance? Have you discovered where he is yet?'

'He's right here, Ellison,' said Clem quietly.

The other swung round with a sudden, jerky movement, his jaw dropping slackly open. Then a gleam came into the close-set eyes and his hands made a swift move towards the guns in his belt, but in that moment, he stopped as the gun in Clem's right hand levelled itself on the other's chest.

'Better not make that kind of move,' warned Clem quietly, 'unless you want to die now. That might upset my plans a little. You see there's some talking you've got to do first. Then I'll decide whether or not to kill you, or turn you over to the decent citizens of this town. I'm quite sure they'll know exactly how to deal with you.'

The other started to bluster and there was a hint of fear at the back of his eyes. 'If you think you'll get away with threatening a law officer, you're badly mistaken, Vance,' he snarled. 'Now put that gun away and come peaceable. You've caused enough trouble in these parts, without doing any more. I promised you a fair trial yesterday, but you didn't take my offer. Mebbe you've thought it over and decided to be reasonable.'

Clem shook his head slowly, grinning tightly. He went forward and seated himself calmly on the edge of the other's desk, staring down into the other's face, noticing the tiny beads of sweat which had popped out on the Sheriff's forehead.

'I never change my mind, especially when it comes to crooked lawmen who hide behind their Star and go in with killers like Mark Heller.' He moved the gun a little so that it pointed directly between the other's eyes. 'Don't try to deny it,' he snapped thinly. 'I know all about those papers in the safe in the wall behind your desk. I went through them very carefully the other night before you came in with Gomez. It seems you're a little too friendly with Heller. The ranchers already know why Heller is holding onto the land up north. They know why he's trying to force them to sell their spreads to him at rock-bottom prices and why he means to shoot it out with them and burn down their ranches if they don't play along with him. And what's more to the point, they're now going to do something about it.'

The Sheriff licked his lips and stared as though mesmerised at the end of the barrel less than two inches from his forehead. 'Now be careful with that gun, Vance. It may go off and you'll get nowhere trying to murder a Sheriff. You know that as well as I do.'

'Don't tempt me, Ellison,' hissed Clem tightly. 'I've met your sort before. You're the lowest scum that ever walked the face of the earth. An honest crook, even a killer I can understand, but a lawman who throws in his lot with murderers while hiding behind his badge is a little more than I can stomach. It would give me the greatest pleasure in the world to pull this trigger. But unfortunately, I need you. You're going to be a star witness in the case against Mark Heller. You've got quite a lot of valuable evidence in that safe of yours and I need it.'

'There's nothing there but a few official documents,' said the other and the fear was now clearly to be seen in his face. 'I refuse to show them to you.'

'You refuse?' There was deliberate menace in Clem's voice now. He rose smoothly forward, getting to his feet, the barrel of the gun never wavered.

'You're not in any position to refuse, Ellison. Either you open that safe and hand over those papers to me or I'll shoot you and do it myself. The choice is yours.'

The other was shaking now. He held out his hands almost pleadingly. 'Heller will kill me if I do,' he said whiningly.

'And I'll kill you now if you don't,' Clem pointed out harshly. He drew back the hammer of the Colt. The click brought more sweat out on the other's face and he rubbed the back of his hand absently across it. 'You wouldn't dare,' he said, trying to convince himself more than Clem. 'The shot would bring everyone running to the office. The town is crawling with men who've been given orders to shoot you on sight.'

'So I've heard,' drawled Clem quietly. 'Trouble is that I managed to get here without being seen or shot at, and I reckon I can go out the same way. And if any of your men are foolish enough to try to trail me out of town, they'll get the same that Heller and his men got when they tried to burn down the Warburg ranch.'

From the look in the Sheriff's eyes, it was obvious that he had heard nothing of what happened to Heller and his crew of picked killers, although he probably knew that the other had ridden off with the intention of destroying the ranch.

'What happened to Heller?' he asked hesitantly. His hands were flat on the top of the desk now, fingers twisting aimlessly, a sure sign that he was more worried than he tried to look.

'He ran into trouble. Mebbe he figured that nobody would dare to oppose him if he rode up in force and demanded what he called his 'rights'.'

Clem paused deliberately, watching the growing fear on the Sheriff's puffy features. 'Only Warburg and his men did fight and in the end, it was Heller who jumped his horse and rode hell for leather off the spread, running like a whipped cur with his tail between his legs. And he'll go on running now, because everybody in the territory will soon know that Heller ain't the big man he's tried to make himself out to be over these past years. He's just a yeller coward who hides behind a show of force. Face up to him and give him a taste of his own medicine and he runs like a dog.'

'You're lyin',' Vance. Heller wouldn't run away from a job like that until he'd finished what he set out to do, and you know it.'

'Reckon you'd better ask him the next time you both meet, somewhere in a jail.' Clem rasped the words out and jabbed across the desk with the gun, the muzzle sinking into the other's paunch so that he hunched himself back in his chair in a vain effort to get away and squealed like a child. Sweat ran down his ashen face, into his eyes, and dropped off his chin as he stared at the gun.

'Now git that safe open and hand me out those papers,' demanded Clem. He waited until the other had stumbled awkwardly to his feet, then moved around the side of the desk and stood close beside him as he fingered the button which opened the panel and then opened the door of the safe.

'You're going to pay for this outrage with your life,' began the other hoarsely, turning to face Clem, but the other merely jabbed him harder with the gun and he turned back quickly, digging his hand inside the cavity in the wall. He brought out the money first and laid it carefully on the desk. Then the bag containing the pieces of gold and lastly the bundle of papers which had first evoked Clem's interest.

'Just official documents,' quavered Ellison throatily, as he laid them down on the desk. 'They're all Government property.'

'Sure,' sneered Clem. 'Like those papers that the homesteaders have, giving them title to the land up north. Only theirs happen to be genuine as the court in Dodge will soon decide. These are all very clever forgeries, signed and witnessed by Gomez and yourself. Even without the murder charges I can bring against you, there ought to be enough evidence here to get you a long prison sentence. I reckon it will be a long time before Senica is cursed with a Sheriff as crooked as you.'

'Now listen,' said the other, pleadingly. 'Don't you think you and I can come to some satisfactory arrangement? After all, there's more gold and treasury notes there than I need. But enough to make you rich for the rest of your life. You could ride out of here, and make yourself a place in California and be as powerful a man there as Heller is here with all that wealth.'

'I wondered when you were going to suggest a deal like that, Ellison,' said Clem harshly. 'And how long do you reckon I'd live even if I did accept your offer. I'd be shot dead before I reached the edge of town and then you'd have your gold and money back and the menace would have been removed. You must take me for a fool. Besides, what's to stop me taking the lot, here and now?'

'Nothing. Take it if you want it, Vance. It's all yours.' The other seemed almost beside himself with terror.

Vance shook his head. 'I'm more interested in ridding the territory of snakes like you and Heller, than in getting this money,' he said thinly. 'Besides, I hear there's quite a big reward out back east for Heller, dead or alive. Might be that I'll claim it myself.'

'You goddarned fool!' Desperately, the Sheriff lunged for his guns, seeking to catch Clem off balance. He was still reaching for them when the slug tore into his chest, the force of it slamming him back against the wall, just below the safe, his arms spread wide. For a second, he hung there in a position of crucifixion, eyes beginning to glaze over. Then the invisible force which seemed to be supporting him broke and he collapsed onto his knees, falling forward so that his head struck the side of the desk with a sickening force.

Clem bent and picked up the papers which the Sheriff had knocked over onto the floor when he had fallen. At the moment, he was not interested in the dollar bills or the gold. He scooped up the papers showing how Heller had taken over control of the land to the north, land on which the railroad company was trying to build their railroad and which Heller had obtained by forgery and thrust them into his shirt. That shot was bound to have been heard by someone on the street and the significance of it would be realised instantly. He had to get out of there and fast, otherwise he would find himself in a trap. He could hear the thudding of boots along the boardwalk in the distance and moved swiftly, opening the door into the passage at the back which led out into the narrow alley along which he had decided to make his escape. He had hoped to take the Sheriff with him, alive. As a hostage, the other would have proved to be extremely useful. Now that he was dead, one of the principal witnesses against Heller was no longer available to him.

As he swung open the door and stepped out into the corridor, hurrying along it to the door at the far end, past the empty cells and their barred doors, he heard the soft tread behind him and half turned, but not soon enough. Something crashed down hard on the back of his skull and he slumped to the floor. The dim sunlight streaming in through the solitary window, the sound of loud, excited voices behind him as someone tried the outer door and shook the handle fiercely; all of this faded and he knew no more.

He was not aware of the man who stooped over him with an expression of sadistic triumph on his swarthy features. He knew nothing of it when the other pouched the gun with which he had knocked Clem unconscious, hooked his hands beneath his armpits and began to drag him towards the door at the rear.

When he did finally return to consciousness and opened his eyes, with a splitting pain creasing the back of his skull, it was to see unfamiliar surroundings, a long deal table and a chair on the other side. A chair in which Gomez sat, the scar on his forehead where Clem's bullet had creased it, still an angry red in the sunlight, a gun pointed directly at Clem's chest.

6

Outlaw Justice

Glancing down, Clem realised that he was bound to the chair in which he sat, unable to move his arms or legs. His guns had been taken away and there was the slickness of blood on the back of his head. He tried to move his head but the pain which shot through his skull held him still.

Gomez gave a low chuckle. 'You thought perhaps, señor, that you could shoot at me as you did and still remain alive? That was foolish. Always, Gomez will wait until the time comes to repay his debt. Perhaps you are wondering why it was that I did not shoot you back there in the Sheriff's office, instead of bringing you all the way out here. Or I could have left you to the crowd when they burst into the jail, looking for the man who had killed their Sheriff.' He shrugged his shoulders almost delicately and fingered the gun in his hand caressingly.

'The truth is that I mean to kill you in a very special way. I will not shoot you as you tried to kill me. By the time I have finished with you, you will be pleading with me to finish you, to make it quick, so that death might come as a release to the agony you will suffer.'

'You're insane,' said Clem tightly, holding himself very still, watching the other's eyes. There was a complete absence of any expression or emotion in them. Then he saw the anger flare up at the back of them and the other leaned his body over the table with the speed of a coiled rattler striking at its intended victim and the butt of the gun struck his left shoulder with a bone-crushing, numbing force. He gasped out aloud with the agony of it as the pain rode swiftly along his arm and even into his curled fingers.

'You should not say such things,' said

the other smoothly. 'For my country-men, revenge is the one thing that must be taken.' He fingered the scar on his forehead, a flaming red weal across the swarthy skin. 'This I shall carry to my grave, but I shall live the rest of my life knowing that the man who did it, died at my hand. You understand do you not, señor?'

'No.' Clem spoke sharply, trying not to show fear. 'You jumped me on the trail, you and that other killer, and tried to bushwhack me. I fired back at you in self-defence.'

'Of course. How forgetful of me.' The other smiled, showing his white teeth. He leaned back in the chair, watching Clem lazily from beneath lowered lids. The other had the impression that the half-breed was deliberately playing with him as a cat would with a mouse. Ignoring the pain in his skull, he tried moving his legs under cover of the table, but the other had tied the knots expertly and he knew that it would be impossible for him to wriggle out of these bonds. It was the same with his hands.

'It is useless to try to escape,' murmured the other silkily. 'The ropes are very tight.' He rose lithely to his feet and walked over to the small window. Clem noticed that there was dust on it, and in the room too. The place had the air of a building which had not been lived in for a very long time. It was probably a house on the outskirts of Senica, although how the other had got him there without being seen by the people running to investigate the shot, was something he did not know.

'What do you intend to do?' he asked finally as the other stood at the window with his back to him. 'Shoot me in the back — like a real man?' He put a note of insolence into his voice, hoping to sting the other into making a mistake. But Gomez did not even turn and it was impossible to see the expression on his face.

'My people have several methods of extracting information from unwilling prisoners, señor. They are all exceedingly painful and, by their means, it takes a long time for the victim to die. I have learned all of these tortures. That is why I am always so useful to Señor Heller. There are times when he must have information and the man refuses to talk. Then he sends for me and it is not long, I assure you, before they are more than willing to tell him everything he wants to know.'

Listening to that smooth, oily voice, Clem knew that the other was telling the truth, that this was no idle boast of his. He wondered what was coming next and at that moment remembered the papers he had thrust into his shirt. Almost of their own accord, his eyes glanced down at his shirt and Gomez, who had turned swiftly, caught the movement and smiled broadly. 'You are worried about the papers which were hidden in the Sheriff's safe, perhaps. Rest assured that they are in an even safer place. You realise that I could not afford to allow you to take them, not with my own name so prominently mentioned on them all. The Sheriff was a fool to keep them there and Heller also for trusting that man with them. He seemed to think that I could not be trusted to keep them in a safe place. Now, perhaps, when he learns of this, he will realise that I was right after all.'

'Seems to me that you're being foolish too, Gomez,' said Clem, forcing evenness into his voice, looking the other straight in the eye. 'There are other papers equally important and pointing also to your guilt. I don't have them and at the moment they are in the right hands. You don't really think that Heller is going to remain alive after tonight, do you?'

Gomez shrugged. 'Whatever happens to Heller after tonight is no concern of mine. I have seen enough of what is happening here. I know that very soon more homesteaders will arrive in the territory and Heller will not be able to fight all of them no matter how many men he pays to ride for him. With the money and gold that the Sheriff so thoughtfully kept in that safe, I shall ride out of here and head west. As soon as I have taken care of you, of course.' His smile was evil as he walked forward.

Clem tensed himself. There was no mistaking the death which showed in the half-breed's eyes as he stalked forward. He had been nursing his anger for a long time now until he saw his chance for revenge. Inwardly, Clem cursed himself for not realising that the other might have been somewhere around the Sheriff's office. His head had cleared now and a little of the strength was flowing back into his body, but it was still impossible to budge the ropes by so much as an inch.

Gomez came closer and seated himself on the edge of the table, looking down at him, a sneering grin on his features. 'How does it feel to have the tables turned on you, Vance?' he murmured. 'It wasn't so bad when you had Sheriff Ellison at the point of a gun, but now the boot is on the other foot. Now it's your turn to plead with me for mercy.'

Clem tightened his lips. He knew only too well what kind of man the other was, a man who revelled in the sadistic pleasure he gained from seeing others suffer. He was determined not to give such pleasure to this man.

'If you're expecting me to plead with you, Gomez, you're wrong,' he said sharply.

'We shall see, señor,' murmured the other. He swung one leg idly and Clem noticed that he had pouched his gun and there was a long, slender-bladed knife in his right hand, the sunlight glinting bluely along the smooth steel. He found himself watching the play of light along it against his will, his head bent back a little until the muscles of his neck corded and began to ache intolerably. Even though he knew what to expect, the other's move was so swift and sudden that he had neither the chance to move nor cry out. The edge of the knife flicked savagely across his cheek, drawing blood. The pain came a second later and it was as if a red-hot needle had been drawn through his skin, stretching it in agony.

The half-breed's lips were drawn back into a thin, hard line now as he leaned forward over the desk, his face very close to Clem's. 'It seems a pity, does it not, that everything has to end this way. Your friends among the nesters and the other ranchers will have to try to get along without you. Whether or not you have given them sufficient leadership, sufficient courage to go through with their plan to attack Heller, I do not know. If you have, then they may succeed. I am a realist, my friend. I do not fight against fate, but allow it to fight for me. By the time the showdown comes, I shall be well on my way west, with enough money and gold to last me a lifetime. Ellison was a fool, keeping all of that wealth hidden away. He knew that he would never get the chance to use it while Heller was still alive. Now, he will never get that chance.'

'And you think that you will, Gomez?'

'I'm certain of it.' The other smiled broadly.

Desperately, without allowing any emotion to enter his face or eyes, Clem tried to hold the other's undivided attention, praying that the half-breed had not heard the soft stealthy footstep outside the building, nor seen the faint, sun-thrown shadow which had appeared briefly against the dusty glass of the window behind him.

'Then you're a far bigger fool than I took you for,' he said sharply, loudly.

'You don't stand a chance of getting out of town alive — and you know it. But all this act you've put on supposedly for my benefit, has been for your own, because you're trying to bolster up your own courage to go out there and try to ride through the ring of men that Heller has placed around Senica. You know as well as I do that he's got men watching every trail for me, to shoot me down on sight. How are you going to explain your presence when you try to ride through them? They'll be mighty suspicious and if they should decide to search you — '

The knife blade flicked again, this time at the back of his neck, drawing more blood. As yet, the cuts were not deep. Gomez laughed harshly, loudly. Then, a moment later, his laugh was cut off and it changed to something else, a horrible, drawn-out gurgle that sent little thrills chasing each other up and down Clem's spine. The half-breed's face contorted into a grimace of agony and his fingers scrabbled aimlessly with the top of the desk as the knife dropped from his hand and landed on the floor at Clem's feet.

At that moment, the other fell forward against Clem's shoulder and he saw the hilt of the knife which stuck out from between the other's shoulder blades. Already, there was a red stain beginning to soak through into his shirt.

247

With an effort, Clem raised his eyes from the dead body still leaning heavily on top of him and looked over it towards the doorway. The door had opened noiselessly and Brad Thorpe stood framed in the opening. He came into the room silently and pulled the half-breed off Clem. Picking his knife from the other's back with an almost nonchalant ease, he wiped it on the half-breed's shirt and then cut through the ropes which bound Clem to the chair.

'It seems I arrived just in time,' said the other in his deep, booming voice. 'This must be the man Gomez you spoke of.'

Clem nodded slowly and stretched his legs, trying to ease the cramp which threatened to tie his muscles in knots. He chafed his wrists where the thin rope had cut into them. 'How did you manage to find me?' he asked tensely.

'Simple. I guessed that you'd pay a visit to the Sheriff and I was outside the office when I heard that shot. I'd seen this character ride up about ten minutes before and slip around to the back and figgered his motives weren't any good. So I was back there watching and saw him drag you out a few moments after the shooting. He put you into the saddle of your own horse and brung you to this place on the edge of town. I wasn't sure whether he was helping you or not, so I decided to listen in on your conversation for a while. When I heard enough, I decided to step in and take a hand.'

'I'm glad that you did. You saved my life.' Clem found his guns and thrust them into their holsters. 'But there's no time to be lost. I've got to get to Warburg's ranch. He's called a meeting of the ranchers in the area for tonight. We're planning to get together and ride against Heller. It's the only way he can be stopped, I'm convinced of that.'

'You'll need help. He's got some men riding in now. My son spotted them in the desert just before I left the camp. That was what I was riding into town to tell you. Thought you might want to know in case you had to change our plans.'

'We may have to. Did he see how many there were?'

'Said he couldn't be sure, but reckoned there were at least thirty, probably more. They were riding hell for leather to the north. Reckons they ought to reach Heller's ranch about now if they kept going like that all the way.'

'Don't worry, they would,' said Clem harshly. There was a growing tightness in his chest. He had the impression that even if he got all of the ranchers and their men together and led them in one big party to Heller's ranch, there might still be too many of the outlaws for them to handle.

'I don't like to ask you to bring your men out into this, Brad,' he said grimly. 'Especially after the way these men attacked your train the other night. And there's still the definite possibility that Heller might have some men to spare and send them out with orders to attack you, knowing you will be practically defenceless.'

'We'll ride with you whenever you're ready,' declared the other tightly. 'We're in this deal just as deeply as those ranchers, probably more so. Heller is trying to cheat us out of land that's rightfully ours.'

'Suit yourselves. I won't say that we don't need you, because we do. If those men of Heller's get to his ranch before we do, then we'll have a big fight on our hands and every gun will come in useful.'

'I'll get the men together and we'll ride out at dusk. Where'll we meet you? At Heller's place?'

'Yeah. After dark. You'll hear shooting if we're there. But whatever happens don't go blundering in if we aren't there. Those killers will shoot you and your men to ribbons. They're just waiting for a chance like that to pick us off in little groups. They know that if we go in in a body, they don't stand much of a chance.'

'We'll be careful,' promised the other. He glanced down at the half-breed's body lying on the floor behind the table. 'What do we do about him?'

'Leave him there,' muttered Clem curtly. 'If any of his friends find him, they'll have to guess who killed him.'

He glanced quickly to right and left as he reached the door, then stepped out into the narrow alley. His sorrel was tethered to a post twenty feet away and the homesteader's horse was standing at the end of the alley. It came to him as Thorpe whistled shrilly.

With an effort, taking a deep breath, Clem clambered up into the saddle and forced his head to clear. Gingerly, he felt the lump on the back of his skull and winced as his fingers touched the wound. For a moment, he swayed in the saddle and Thorpe looked at him with an expression of concern on his bearded features. 'Think you can make it all right, Clem. You don't look too good to me. That knock on the head didn't help things.'

'I'll make it all right,' he said, gritting his teeth. 'I've got to. If I don't show up at that cattlemen's meeting, they may never pluck up enough courage to fight and if they don't seize this chance, they may never get another. Heller knows that he had to tighten his control over the territory, or he's finished for good. With those men riding up from the south, he'll still have a big enough army of hired killers and gunslammers to rule this place.'

'Then if you're sure, I'll warn the others.' The other hesitated for a moment, then wheeled his horse sharply and cantered off down the narrow alley. At the end, he paused for a moment, turned and glanced back, then gave a wave of his right hand, and vanished out of sight.

Clem rode slowly through the alley and out of town. His head still hurt and an occasional wave of dizziness made it difficult for him to think properly or keep his hold on the reins. Several times, it seemed he would have to halt and get down, to rest up for a while, but the knowledge that the sands of time were running out swiftly and that it was nearly sundown, drove him on, up to the limit of human endurance.

Things grew spotty in front of him as the sorrel jogged on, skirting most of the trails and cutting across rough, open country. Fortunately, details didn't spin or fade out completely and he was able to keep a grip on his senses. Shortly before nightfall he reached the narrow river that ran through the Warburg spread and although it wasted a few minutes, he climbed weakly from the saddle, walked forward to the river bank, and plunged his hands into the cold water up to the elbows. Then he gathered it in his cupped hands and threw it into his face. It struck him coldly and ran down into his shirt but his head began to clear and he could think properly now. Some of the strength was shocked back into his limbs by the cold water. He drank deeply of it, felt better and climbed back more quickly into the saddle, urging the horse forward into the darkness of coming night.

He noticed that there were lights burning in the windows of the Warburg ranch as he topped the low rise and set the mount at the trail which led down into the small courtyard. There were several horses tethered to the rail and more inside the corral than he remembered. He noticed, too, that several milling around inside the corral were saddled and guessed that Warburg had been true to his word and had got the message to most of the other ranchers, telling them to be there at sundown.

He entered the ranch and Warburg met him in the hallway, giving him a quick nod. There was a relieved look on his face. 'Glad you managed to get here, Clem,' he said quickly. 'I heard that there'd been trouble in town. One of the ranchers heard that the Sheriff had been shot and that the townfolk were trying to get the man who did it.

They swear that he must've escaped out the back way, because nobody saw him leave. That wouldn't have been you, would it?'

Clem nodded grimly. 'I shot Ellison, if that's what you mean, Clint. He had the papers we need, offered to split his money and gold with me and when I refused, he went for his gun. I had no other choice. Then somebody slugged me in the corridor just as I was making my getaway. When I came to, I'd lost the papers and had been taken to some place on the outskirts of Senica by Gomez.'

'That half-breed.' There was a note of tension in the other's voice. He sounded momentarily alarmed. 'I knew that he was after you, determined to kill you after what you did the other day. But how did you get away?'

'Brad Thorpe, one of the nesters who rode into town a few days ago, spotted Gomez taking me away across his horse and followed him. He knifed Gomez when he tried some of his fancy tricks on me to get me to talk.'

'Then the half-breed is dead?'

'That's right. Thorpe has gone back to their camp to get some men together. I figured if we were going to attack Heller tonight, we would need as many men as we could get. I'm not sure whether or not the townsfolk will be swayed to his side now that Ellison is dead. They may. He can be quite eloquent when he tries and he still has some kind of hold over them. Even if they decide to keep out of this, that it's no concern of theirs what Heller does with us, we've still got to take into account that band he sent south with the cattle they rustled. They've been spotted heading back to the ranch.'

'So soon.' The other rubbed his chin thoughtfully. 'I figured we might have been able to get this finished with before they showed up. This puts a different light onto things.'

'You figger that the men in there,' he jerked his thumb in the direction of the front room, through the door of which he could hear the low murmur of voices, 'that they won't ride with us if they know this force has arrived to reinforce Heller?'

'It's possible. These men are in an ugly mood. It's a pity Gomez took those other papers from you, but at least I've already shown them those you took from the surveyor's office and they're mostly convinced that Heller is at the back of all this rustling. But they won't ride out with us unless they're sure that they stand a good chance of defeating him.'

'Then I don't want you to mention these other men at all,' said Clem decisively.

'You mean you're not going to let them know what they're heading into?' There was a note of incredulity in the other's tone.

'That's right. I know you may think they have a right to know, but I'm equally convinced that we have to fight Heller tonight, or we never shall.'

'Well, I don't know. It's taking one hell of a risk.'

'Good God, man, if we don't take risks we'll get nowhere. We've got Heller on the run now. We have to force home our advantage, give him no time to pull himself together. We can beat him, I know we can.'

The other pondered the question for a moment, then nodded in reluctant agreement. 'Very well then, I won't say a word to the others about it.'

'Fine. Now let's go in and try to convince them that we can defeat Heller.'

★ ★ ★

The front room of the ranch was filled almost to overflowing with grim, sun-bronzed faces that turned and regarded Clem with curiosity as he entered with Warburg. He noticed that almost every one of them carried a gun. They looked hard and determined men, thought Clem, but how many of them were prepared to risk their lives to end this menace, this reign of terror under which they had suffered for so long? That was the all-important question and it was up to him to persuade them that this was now the only course open to them, that unless they fought Heller in the only way he understood, with guns and bullets, they would be ground into dust and their land taken over under their very noses. How many Heller would allow to remain alive was a debatable point.

Clem knew few of the men standing or sitting in front of him. All that he did know about them was that they were in trouble and, whether they knew it or not, they were looking to him to help them. It seemed strange, he mused inwardly, that he had ridden into this territory for only one reason, to kill Mark Heller and those of his men who had ridden with him on that fateful day when Sheriff Peterson had been shot down in cold blood in the street in Carson City. Now, although it had been no wish of his, he seemed to have become the central figure in a territory-wide drama at whose magnitude he had been unable to guess when he had first come here.

There was the sound of horses outside and he saw some of the men reach purposefully for their guns. Then the outer door opened and two more men came in, nodded greeting to those in the room and stood against the far wall. One grey-haired and sallow-skinned, mopped his face with a blue bandana and nodded to Warburg.

Clint cleared his throat, looked around the assembled men, then said quietly: 'Well, I reckon that we're all here now so I'll explain the real reason why we're gathered here tonight.' There was a tense and expectant silence in the room as the others waited for him to go on.

'You all know that we've been losing cattle over the past three or four months to this band of rustlers who've been moonlighting our beef out of the territory and herding it down south to the border. So far, we've only had our suspicions as to who might be at the back of it, but now, thanks to Clem Vance here, we now have positive proof that it is Mark Heller and his men. We've now got to organise ourselves and drive Heller and his hired killers clear out of the territory, before he gets any more guns on his side. Clem here figures that if we strike tonight, before Heller has a chance to get his men ready, and while a good part of them are still south with our beef, we stand a good chance of finishing this for good. But we have to ride together. I know how you feel about the nesters who've arrived in Senica with bills of sale from the Government. We don't like 'em here. They cut up the range and parcel it into little lots and generally make a nuisance of themselves. But they've offered to throw in their guns alongside ours and I say that we should let them ride with us. Heller is our big enemy now. Not the homesteaders. We can't fight the Government and hope to win out in the end.'

There was a low mutter from some of the men in the corner of the room, but no one stood up to argue the point.

Clem moved forward. 'You've all seen those papers I took from the surveyor's office. They tell you why Heller wants to keep that land. The railroad, if it runs through here, will be an enormous boon to all of you ranchers. It means that there'll be a railhead close by Senica where you can take your cattle and ship them off back east without having to drive them over some of the worst land in the whole country. By the time they get east, how much of them is skin and bone because of that long drive? Answer me that one.'

'Heller has cattle on his spread. Why doesn't he want the railroad if it's as good a thing as you say it is?' called one of the men.

'We didn't come here to argue about the advantages of the railroad,' called Warburg quickly, 'but to — '

'It's all right, Clint,' said Clem quietly. 'I'll answer him. Heller doesn't want the railroad here for two main reasons. First, I reckon if you care to check on it, you'll find he has scarcely any cattle up there in that valley everyone seems to know about but nobody has ever seen. But more to the point, if the railroad comes through Senica, as it will, then it will bring law and order with it. Pinkerton men, Wells Fargo detectives and, most of all, Sheriffs and Marshals who won't bow down to Mark Heller, accept his bribes and allow him to run this place as he likes. He knows that once this is no longer a frontier town, his reign of power is over.'

The man who had asked the question nodded slowly to himself, apparently satisfied with the answers.

Another said: 'I don't like the idea of riding with sodbusters. How do we know they won't turn on us once we've finished off Heller?'

'You don't,' snapped Clem tightly.

'But if you want their help, then you have no other choice. Besides, I've seen those land deeds that they bought back east from the Government. All of them are for land on the Heller spread. You won't stand to lose anything by their being here.'

The men talked among themselves for some time, then finally one of them, a tall, hatchet-faced man, rose to his feet and looked Clem right in the eye. 'We've decided,' he said harshly. 'We'll get our men together and ride with you. But if those nesters give us any trouble when all this is over, they'll regret it.'

'That seems fair enough,' agreed Clem and heaved a sigh of relief. 'Then I reckon we'd better saddle up. There'll be a moon shortly after midnight and we want to be in position before then. The nesters will join us after dark on Heller's spread. Keep your eyes open for them when you ride in. I don't want to have the wrong folk get shot and warn Heller that we're going for him.'

He waited while they filed out of the

room, went for their horses in the courtyard or the corral and saddled up. A few minutes later, they rode off, each going in his own direction. Clem watched them leave and knew that when they came back they would bring men with them, men ready to fight so that they might continue to live on the range without fear.

'You'd better come back into the house and I'll get something fixed for you to eat, Clem,' said Warburg. 'You look tuckered out. I'll have a look at that lump on the back of your head. Reckon that must've been where Gomez hit you?'

'That's right.' Clem followed the other into the ranch, lowered himself into the chair that the rancher indicated. While food was being prepared, Warburg examined the wound on the back of his head, washing it gently, his hands as expert as any doctor's.

'When you've ridden the range as long as I have, you get so that you're able to handle wounds like this.

Gunshot and knife wounds. Otherwise, you might lose half of your men when you're out there in the middle of the prairie and fifty miles from the nearest sawbones.'

When he had finished, Clem's head felt a little easier and the pain had subsided into a dull ache. He seated himself in front of the table as the food was brought in, helped himself to the potatoes, sweet corn and chicken which Warburg piled onto his plate. He washed it down with hot coffee and felt better when he had finished, leaning back in his chair. Now he had the feeling that he could tackle anything.

'I'll bring in the rest of my men,' said Warburg, getting to his feet. 'I warned them to be ready to ride out.'

There were close on fifteen men in the bunch that rode with Clem and Warburg when they left the ranch and headed out onto the trail which would bring them to the Heller spread. The moon had not yet risen and there was a cool wind blowing from the north into their faces as they rode tall in the saddle. Clem let it blow over him and felt some of the weariness leaving his body. The stars were out in their thousands over their heads, giving a little light to see by.

For most of the way they rode in silence, only the muffled tread of their mounts breaking the clinging stillness of the prairie. As he rode, up in the lead with Clint Warburg, Clem could feel some of the old excitement coming back into his body. At last, he felt that the end was near for Heller and he was determined that his should be the bullet which put an end to the other's vicious and evil life. But most of all, he wanted Heller to know who it was who killed him — and why. He had to be forced to remember Sheriff Peterson and to realise, in the moment before he died, that this was an act of retribution. He had made it clear to Warburg and the other ranchers, that as far as Heller was concerned, he was his. That was all he asked for what he was doing to help them.

At a sharply-angled bend in the river, they met up with two other groups of men who swung in on either side of them. It was difficult to estimate how many there were, but they made a goodly bunch and if they fought well, they stood a good chance of winning through.

More joined them further along the trail and as they rode up to the boundary fence of Heller's spread, Brad Thorpe and the homesteaders rode up to join them. In all, Clem estimated that they had close on seventy men, all armed, all determined to fight for their rights.

The moon was coming up as they broke down the fence and rode roughshod over it, giving a flood of yellow light by which they could see for close on two miles. The spread lay in front of them, quiet and seemingly deserted, but that was only a surface appearance and every man knew that somewhere out there, Heller and his men would be waiting. Clem took in a deep breath of the cool night air and set his face resolutely towards the north. By the time they came within sight of Mark Heller's ranch, the moon would be well up giving them plenty of light, but making it difficult for anyone down there to spot them until it was too late.

He hoped that the men would hold their fire until he gave the word. If one man fired out of turn, it could give away their position before they were set for the attack. They rode over a long, razor-backed ridge in the moonlight, long shadows moving with them and followed a zigzag trail that seemed to stretch for miles in front of them. As he rode, he tried not to think of what might happen if they did not succeed in their task this night. They would never get a second chance to destroy this man. But that was something in the future and he tried to put the thought out of his head. Such ideas only served to slow down a man's reflexes to danger point when the time came for quick and instant action. He moistened his lips and glanced about him at the rest of the men, riding sober-faced in the flooding moonlight, some carrying their rifles ready, others with Colts stuck into their belts or in their holsters. How many men would Hiller have at the ranch? he wondered tensely. It was just possible that they had beaten the others coming from the south, although he doubted it, unless Heller was playing this clever, and he had figured out what they might do and had given orders that the men should remain out there in the desert country and only move in slowly after dark, so as to be able to fall on their rear once the going got tough. The more he reflected on that point, the more logical it seemed. After all, he told himself fiercely, Heller had been with the Southern Army during the war and had fought well for part of the battle. He would know the advantage of having men in reserve to fall upon his enemy's rear and thereby turning the tide of the battle at the crucial moment.

That meant that there might only be a relatively small number guarding the ranch itself. But even so, they would fight like cornered rattlers.

Gradually, as they rode deeper into Heller's spread, the terrain began to change. The low, stunted bushes gave way to tall willows that were saplings at first, then seemed to grow taller and fuller in foliage until it was impossible to tell one year's growth from the next. Underfoot, the bare rock was hidden now in most places by moss and lush grass as the land passed through stale, rocky desert and then into thick woodland, scattered woods of dogwood and gum, before widening out in front of them into the wide, open rangeland.

Scarcely a single word was spoken during the whole of that night ride. Each man seemed to be deeply engrossed in his own thoughts and Clem wondered how many of them were thinking things over now that the time had almost come, and deciding that perhaps they had made a mistake when they had agreed to come out here to fight.

Clint Warburg rode suddenly close to him and said sharply: 'About another mile, Clem. Over that rise there. No sign of any of Heller's men yet. Think he could have gone out to attack one of the other ranches, believing that we'd never attack him?'

'I doubt it. He must know by now that we've been gathering men from all over the territory. And he can guess why we've been doing it. He'd never leave the ranch here unprotected if he thought there was the slightest chance that we might ride in and attack.'

'I hope you're right. If you aren't, then this whole attack might fail completely. Everything depends on catching him here before he's prepared.'

Fifteen minutes later, they climbed the low rise which stood directly to the south of Heller's ranch and stood looking down at it in the dimness. Clem sat tensed in his saddle with a curious expectancy in his mind. At any moment, he expected to hear the sound of gunfire from down there as he and the others were spotted against the skyline, but the silence continued thick and ominous and unbroken.

He drew in a deep breath. 'We'll split into two groups,' he said tersely. 'And ride down and surround the place. This time, I don't want Heller to jump his horse and make a getaway. If any man catches up with him, remember that I want him alive. The rest of those killers are yours to do with as you think fit. But I want Heller.'

'You sure must hate him real bad,' said one of the men wonderingly. 'I'd hate to be in his boots when you catch up with him.'

'I'm going to make him wish that he'd never been born,' said Clem grimly. His fingers twitched convulsively for a moment almost as if he had the other's neck in his hands. Then he forced himself to relax, sitting upright in the saddle. 'Let's move,' he said thickly. 'And remember, I want no shooting until you hear my first shot. Understand?'

There were low murmurs of assent from the assembled men. A moment later, one group rode off into the trees and then down through the thick, succulent grass which lay yellow in the moonlight, circling the ranch to take the outlaws from the rear. Clem waited until he judged they had time to get into position, then gave the other men the order to spread out and move in.

7

The Big Showdown

Everything was ominously quiet in the moonlight as they set their horses to a trot, edging down the hillside towards the Heller ranch. Clem could feel the tension among the men beginning to grow as they drew closer and still not a shot was fired from the ranch. Lights burned yellow in several of the windows and there were plenty of horses milling around in the big corral. He steadied himself in the saddle, holding his body tautly upright, ready for the slightest sign of danger. Everything about this set-up smelled of a trap. Heller was not so much of a fool that he would leave the entire place empty of fighting men and totally unguarded.

As they drew nearer, the men began to spread out until a large half-moon of men were riding up on the ranch-house.

Brad Thorpe edged his way slowly towards Clem and said in a hoarse whisper: 'I've seen many a trap in my lifetime, Clem and this has the same feel about it.'

Clem bit his lip. 'That's what's been annoying me too,' he admitted wryly. 'I've got the feel of eyes boring into me already.'

He eased the sixes in their holsters. Now they were less than two hundred yards from the ranch. There was a small group of aspens fronting the house itself and they dismounted there out of sight from anyone watching from the windows. Clem sensed the men staring at him in the cool darkness under the trees, waiting for him to give the prearranged signal to go in to the attack. Moving swiftly to the edge of the trees, he studied the situation. There was no sense in rushing into this blindly without first surveying the lie of the land. There was an open space of almost a hundred yards between their aspen cover and the front of the house itself, with the squat, low-roofed bunkhouse about fifty yards further on and to one side.

In the vast area of this courtyard there was not a single shrub or bush to give them shelter from gunfire aimed at them from the windows.

Very slowly, he worked his way out into the open for a better look. By now, the rest of his force should have circled the ranch without being spotted and be in a position around the back, ready to move in at his signal. The fact that not a shot had been fired so far indicated that they had done this unseen and unheard. Swiftly, he surveyed the area in the moonlight. The bunkhouse also showed a light or two in the windows along one side. There could be men in there too, which meant he would have to watch both directions at once for fear of leading his men into a position where they could be fired upon from both sides.

More than ever before, the feeling was strong within him that things had happened too easily for this to be anything but a trick on Heller's part, a ruse to entice them closer to the ranch, out into the open and away from any cover. He raised his Colt to fire three swift shots in the air as the signal to the waiting men, crouched down out of sight behind their rifles and sixes but before he could squeeze the trigger, a rifle barked savagely from one of the windows of the ranch and the slug tore the leaves from the branches close to Clem's head as he drew back sharply under cover, cursing himself for being such a downright fool and exposing himself so openly in the moonlight. Sharp eyes had obviously been watching from the ranch. He must have been an excellent target for that marksman, he reflected angrily.

As he lifted the long-barrelled Colt, Heller's voice reached him from one of the windows loud and insolent: 'All right, Vance. We know that you are out there. This is just a warning that all of you men are trespassing on my land. I'm well inside the law if I start shooting now. For me, this is a matter of self-defence. Now tell those men with you to mount up, turn around and ride off my spread. I promise that nothing will happen to any of them just because they rode with you out of an idea of mistaken loyalty. I'm not the kind of man to bear a grudge.'

'That sure is mighty big of you Heller.' Warburg's voice came harshly from the trees just behind Clem. 'You think anybody here is going to believe a word of what you say after you tried your damnedest to kill me and burn my ranch?'

'Listen Warburg.' There was a note of anger in the other's smooth voice now. 'I offered you a fair price for that tumble-down place you call a ranch. It's a better bargain than you ever deserved. If you refused, that was up to you and you deserved everything you got.'

'Don't forgit that we're in on this deal too,' yelled Brad Thorpe sharply. 'You ain't cheating us out of the land we bought legally from the Government back east.'

For a long moment there was silence from the ranch. Clem could guess what Heller was going to try to do. Try to split them by offering one group help and security in return for giving up this idea and riding back to their own places; and the trouble was, Clem thought tightly, that some of these smaller ranchers were almost at the wavering stage already. He might also be trying to stall for time until the rest of his men got there from the desert and possibly more than even up the numbers.

'I figgered that you goddarned sodbusters would come riding in with Vance. Anything to make trouble. That's all you're good for.' For a moment, Clem thought that he denoted a note of desperation in the other's voice but he could not be sure. 'Do you cattlemen seriously reckon that you're going to gain anything by throwing in your lot with Vance and these nesters? You know as well as I do that there are hordes more of them riding into Senica in the next few weeks and they'll all come with these Government deeds entitling them to the land that you have worked and settled for thirty or forty years. Pretty soon, unless you get wise to yourselves and fight them off, you'll be driven off this range altogether. The Government in Washington is backing them to take away your land — not just mine. Surely you can see that. I know they say they only want my land at first, but that's only the start of it. Where is it all going to end?'

'A pretty speech,' called Clem tightly, 'but you ain't convincing anyone here. You've rustled too many head of cattle and killed too many men.' He fired three quick shots into the air. The small ranchers could easily be swung over by this kind of persuasive talk.

The thunder of gunfire ripped across

the cool night air. Windows were shattered into glistening fragments that caught the moonlight for an instant, then vanished along the whole front of the house. The lights went out in every room. Guns poked through the splintered openings, returning the fire. Clem tried to judge from the volume of fire which came from the ranch and the bunkhouse, how many men Heller had down there altogether, in defence of his ranch. There seemed to be plenty of fire coming from the bunkhouse, he could make out the brief orange flashes from the muzzles of the rifles; but even so, it seemed unlikely that the rustling party had got back yet.

That posed another problem. He whirled and plunged back into the trees until he found Brad Thorpe crouched down behind one of the tall aspens, using his rifle to deadly effect.

'Brad, I've a feeling that the party of hombres you spotted earlier today heading here across the desert flats aren't down there with Heller, either inside the ranch or the bunkhouse. That means only one thing. Heller is trying to pull a fast one on us. They must still be out there to the south of us, riding this way hell for leather. I want a man on top of the hill yonder to keep a sharp look out for them. We don't want to run the risk of being taken by surprise.'

'I'll go,' said the other quickly, heaving himself to his feet.

Clem shook his head. 'No. You're too good a shot to lose right now. Send one of your men out there. Preferably one who can make out a rustling party in this tricky moonlight for two or three miles. The more warning we have, the better. Above all, I don't want to be caught between two walls of fire.'

He clapped the other's shoulder as the homesteader slipped away into the darkness of the tangled undergrowth. When he came back a few minutes later, he nodded quickly. 'Bart will watch for you from the top of the hill,' he said thinly. 'He's a good man, keen-sighted. He won't make the mistake of thinking that a shadow is the party.'

'Good. I'm expecting them to try us from the rear as soon as the going gets tough for Heller. If we can break him before the others get here, then I doubt if they'll be any danger. Without Heller to lead them, they'll turn and run for their lives, I'm pretty sure of that.'

'Reckon we won't get far shooting at 'em from this distance,' said the other quietly. 'We'll stand a better chance of smoking 'em out if we rush the ranch from all sides, get to close quarters with the polecats.'

'We'll have to take the bunkhouse first. If we try to rush the ranch, we'd come under heavy fire from there. They could hit us easily without exposing themselves. Get some of them men together and we'll hit the bunkhouse.'

'Now you're talking my kinda language,' gritted the other. There was a look of almost feral anticipation in his deep-set eyes. He moved off into the trees, came back a little while later with ten men close behind him. They had discarded their rifles for six-guns.

'We're all ready to go, Clem,' said Thorpe gruffly. 'I've warned the rest of the men in the trees to give us covering fire as we go in.'

'Once we take the bunkhouse, the others can move up into fresh positions while we force those coyotes inside the ranch to keep their heads down.'

Presently, they broke cover, snaking forward through the tall grass which lay as a narrow fringe on the border of the aspen grove, then out into the open. Slugs whined in murderous ricochet off the hard ground around them as they darted for the bunkhouse. One man, lunging forward at Clem's side, suddenly uttered a harsh grunt of agony and collapsed onto his face. Out of the corner of his eye, Clem saw that he had been hit in the top of the leg, but there was no time to pause and see how badly the other had been hit. He ran on, hearing the vicious, hornet-hum of bullets zipping through the air close to his head. Miraculously, he remained unhurt and a few moments later, he had flung himself forward against the side of the bunkhouse, breathless with the exertion, both sixes in his hands. With an effort, he pulled air down into his heaving, aching lungs. A smashing volley crashed out from the direction of the ranch and he heard Heller's harsh voice yelling orders as the cattle boss spotted this new move on their part and realised that it could mean the end for the men in the bunkhouse.

Carefully, Clem twisted and heaved himself up onto his elbows. The other men came running across the open space and dropped down beside him. Halfway along the side of the bunkhouse, Thorpe had thrown himself down and was already firing at the ranch, his bullets finding their targets as he placed them with a deadly precision.

Three feet from where Clem lay, a window smashed into fragments as one of the outlaws inside smashed at it with the butt of his pistol. Clem caught a fragmentary glimpse of the barrel as the other thrust it out and tried to bring it to bear on one of the men crouched almost directly beneath the window. Without pausing to think, Clem lifted himself up to his full height, heedless of the slugs from the ranch which crashed into the wall of the bunkhouse beside him. The man behind the window uttered a high-pitched yell as Clem fired. At that range, it was impossible to miss. There was a low thud as the other's body hit the floor inside.

Swiftly, Clem ran around to the side of the bunkhouse, calling on the rest of the men to back him up. Kicking in the door savagely, he strode inside, guns blazing in his hands, pumping up and down as he fired shot after shot at the shadows which ran and crouched in front of him as the outlaws tried to get under cover, out of range of that deadly fire. One man rose up to his full height and came charging directly towards

Clem, uttering a savage, bull-like roar at the top of his voice. He was a veritable giant of a man and in the dimness, he seemed even larger than he really was. Clem waited until he came within two feet of him before squeezing the trigger. The Colt bucked against his wrist and the man slithered to a sudden halt, his hands clasped convulsively across his stomach. He hesitated for a moment as though an invisible fist had slammed him hard on the point of the jaw. Then he pitched forward and crashed to the floor at Clem's feet, his body quivering slightly.

The men behind Clem came pouring into the bunkhouse, firing from the hip. Everything seemed noise and confusion. Flashes from the muzzles of their guns lit the long room with brief splashes of light. For a moment there came a few ragged shots from the far end of the bunkhouse, then there was silence in the room. Carefully, Clem went forward, eyes now accustomed to the darkness, until he was sure that every one of the men inside there had been killed.

There was a tensed feeling in his body now like a coiled spring waiting to unwind. Shots were still coming from the ranch where Heller and the rest of his men were holding out.

Now that they had established a vantage point, he was determined to press home his advantage as quickly as possible before those rustlers added their firepower to Heller's already depleted forces. Swiftly, he crammed fresh cartridges into the chambers of his Colts. Then he moved over to one of the windows facing the ranch and came back into the fire just as Brad Thorpe hurled his last shot at the ranch. Carefully, he raised his head above the level of the ledge. From that distance, it was possible to make out details of the ranch and occasionally see the heads of the men as they lifted them to fire.

He snapped two quick shots at one man and saw him reel back away from the window. Thorpe came back into the fight, his face fixed and grim, the battle light still visible in his eyes. 'We've got the varmints on the run now,' he said thickly. 'If they had any sense they'll surrender now before we kill them all.'

Clem grinned tightly. 'They'll never do that,' he answered. 'Most of those men in there with Heller are either killers or men who rode with him when he was with Quantrill's Raiders during the war. They're all wanted by various states on some charge or other. Reckon they know that rope's waiting for them if they do get caught. So they'd rather die fighting than swing. Heller knows that. That's why he hired them in the first place. He knows he can rely on them to fight to the last bullet.'

Clem gave his orders to the men in low, clear, steady tones. Three of the homesteaders had been hit by the fire when they had burst into the bunk-house and two were lying on a couple of beds against one wall, out of range of any slugs from the ranch. One was groaning continually, a bullet in his left knee where the bone had been smashed. The other two were quiet, but Clem was not sure as far as these men were concerned, whether or not this was a good sign. He began to wish that they had brought Doc Birkett with them, but he had been needed back there in the trees where he was not only tending to the more seriously wounded, but was also handling a rifle as well. For a man who believed only in saving life, thought Clem inwardly, Doc Birkett was proving himself to be an excellent shot with a high-powered Winchester.

A sudden yell from one of the men watching the far window, swung Clem round sharply. He hurried across the room, keeping his head low as bullets hummed and smashed into the woodwork.

'What is it?' He demanded hastily.

The other pointed. In the bright moonlight, Clem could just make out the running figure, heading across the courtyard in their direction. The man ran crabwise, bobbing and weaving from side to side to present a more difficult target to the men in the ranch who were doing their best to cut him down before he could reach cover. Bullets skipped about his feet as he ran.

Without turning his head to take his eyes off the man, Clem yelled to the men on the opposite side of the bunkhouse. 'Keep firing! Force those outlaws to keep their heads wells down.' He knew with a sick certainty that the running man would never make it unless they did and it was equally obvious that the man was coming with important news otherwise he would have stayed under cover among the trees. The crash of gunfire increased savagely in volume as the men responded to his call.

The man was now less than fifty yards away and still miraculously on his feet. He plunged headlong for another ten yards then staggered as a bullet hit him. Another got him in the shoulder, spinning him round under the shattering force of the impact. His legs seemed to buckle beneath him as though no longer able to bear the weight of his body, and he fell, sprawling full length in the moonlight.

Clem reached the door of the bunkhouse in three rapid strides and jerked it open savagely. Before any of the others could make a single move to stop him, he was outside in the yellow moonlight, the thunder of gunfire hammering at his ears, as he raced towards the wounded man.

A couple of bullets hummed and hit the dirt beside him, whining into the night with a thin, high-pitched wail of sound. Clem ignored them, threw himself down beside the wounded man who was trying desperately to pull himself along the ground.

'More men . . . they're . . . ' The other spoke in gasps as spasms of agony bit into his twisted body. He tried to lift himself as though to point back in the direction from which he had come, but Clem stopped him.

'That'll all have to wait until I get

you under cover,' he said tersely. Pushing himself up onto his knees, he lifted the other across his shoulders and started towards the bunkhouse. Once, the man cried out with the pain of his wounds as Clem carried him swiftly back under cover, staggering in through the bunkhouse door and laying the man down on the nearest bunk.

'That sure was some damned fool thing to do,' rasped Thorpe. 'You might easily have been killed out there.'

'So might he,' retorted Clem tightly. He ripped the blood-soaked cloth away from the wound in the man's shoulder. The last bullet had penetrated the fleshy part of his body and although it was bleeding profusely and would undoubtedly be exceedingly painful it looked more dangerous than it really was.

'We'll get Doc Birkett to take a look at that wound of yours as soon as we've smoked those polecats out of the ranch,' he said. 'You'd better lie still meantime though, that bullet is still in there somewhere and I reckon he'll have to probe for it.'

The man nodded weakly. 'Had to get here to warn you,' he muttered. His lips were curled back over his teeth with pain and his voice was so low and feeble that Clem had to lean forward over the bunk to pick out the words: 'Bart spotted those rustlers in the draw out there on the edge of the spread. They're coming up fast. About thirty of them, he estimates. Reckons they'll hit us in five, mebbe ten minutes.'

'Don't worry, we'll take care of 'em.' Clem forced conviction into his voice. He had been expecting this move and one of the reasons he had been so determined to capture the bunkhouse had been to give the men on the hillside, in the aspen grove, a breathing space in which to take care of this new menace. Here, he reasoned, it ought to be possible, with the men he had with him, to take care of the outlaws in the ranch. He left the man lying on the bunk and went over to Brad Thorpe.

The nester turned and looked at him speculatively. 'I had an idea that this would happen,' he muttered harshly. 'What chance you reckon we have now? Casualties have been pretty heavy on both sides and it ain't going to be easy to fight off thirty or so fresh men.'

'I know. I reckon if we can take care of Heller and those other hombres in the ranch out there, Warburg and the rest should be able to take care of that other party.'

'I hope you're right. We're running pretty short of ammunition.' 'He checked the gunbelt around his waist.

'We'll make it,' gritted Clem. 'If we don't it will mean the end of everything.' He snapped a quick shot at a dark, shadowy figure that appeared briefly in the porch of the ranch. The man yelled and dropped back out of sight. The sound of heavy gunfire came from the top of the hill and against the brilliant moonlight Clem could make out the flashes of gunfire.

'Can you hear me in there, Vance?'

Heller's voice reached Clem clearly even above the racket of gunfire.

He eased himself close to the window, not exposing himself for fear of a trick. 'I can hear you, Heller. What do you want? To give yourself up?'

'Not at all. You must have heard that firing out there on the hill. Those are my men up there who've just ridden in from the desert. Your men don't stand a chance now. Better throw down your guns and come out with your hands high. There's been enough killing for one night, I reckon.'

'The killing will stop when you and the rest of your gunslingers are dead,' Clem called back.

'You're being a stubborn fool,' screamed the other. A pause, then: 'The rest of you men in there. Don't listen to Vance or the homesteaders. They're simply wanting you to do their fighting for them. They're too damned scared to fight this battle themselves, they have to get you ranchers to do it for them. My quarrel is only with Vance and the nesters. The rest of you throw down your guns and come out, I promise you there'll be no retribution.'

A fusillade of shots greeted his remarks. Clem leaned back and checked the slugs in his Colts. There were pitifully few of them left now. True they had killed several of the outlaws, but time was running against them now. Somehow, they had to rush the ranch, co-ordinate their attack with that of the men to the rear of the large building, and get to grips with the outlaws. But from the bunkhouse, the ranch itself looked virtually impregnable.

He called the rest of the men together. 'We've got to go in there and smoke them out quickly,' he rasped. 'Nothing will be gained by sitting here and sniping at them whenever they show themselves. Heller knows that pretty soon we'll be out of ammunition and that's all he's waiting for. He can afford to bide his time and then rush us.'

'Just give the word and we'll move in on them, Clem,' said Thorpe fiercely.

'Once we're inside the ranch, shoot down every man you see, but remember that I want Heller.'

They nodded in agreement, edged their way towards the door. Seconds later, one of the wounded men on the bunk at the far end of the room, lifted himself up suddenly and yelled: 'What's that out there, lighting up the sky?'

Clem whirled, raced to the nearest window and peered out. For a moment, he stared in numbed bewilderment at the scene in front of him. Then he swung back to face the others. 'They've fired the grass out there and the wind is bringing the flames in this direction. They're trying to burn us out.'

The others crowded around him and Clem knew instinctively why Heller had held their attention for the past few moments, to allow the fire to take a firm hold before they were aware of it. Not that they could do much about it, thought Clem quickly, his mind whirling inside his head. Every gun in the ranch would be trained on the bunkhouse now, with itchy fingers on the triggers, ready to shoot them down like rats the instant they ran out into the open. He drew in a deep breath. The grass out there, knee-high and dried by long weeks of scorching sun, blazed savagely, the wall of flame advancing with a terrible swiftness towards the bunkhouse. Although there was an open space of perhaps ten yards on one side of the building, there was little doubt in his mind that, driven by the wind, the flames would leap that and engulf the wooden bunkhouse.

'There's only one chance left to us,' he said tightly. It was a dangerous plan that had formed in his mind. 'We've got to wait here until the fire reaches us. By that time, there ought to be enough smoke around to provide us with the shield we need to run across to the ranch. Those polecats in there don't know it, but they've sealed their own fate.'

'You think there's a chance?' asked Thorpe harshly. Without waiting for an answer, he nodded towards the three men in the bunks. 'And what about these men? We can't leave them here to be burned alive.'

'While the rest of us head for the ranch, I want three men to take these men back to the trees. You ought to make it while we keep the others busy.'

By now, it was possible to make out the vicious crackling of the flames as they swept down the hillside, closer to the bunkhouse which lay directly in their path. The three seriously wounded men had been lifted from the bunks and the men stood ready to carry them to safety. Already, black smoke was beginning to pour in through the shattered windows.

Clem held his breath. It was going to be touch and go. Smoke was beginning to filter between them and the ranch. Another minute or so and it would be impossible for the outlaws to see them. This was the moment he was waiting for. A wave of heat swept down on them as they crouched near the door and several of the men were coughing violently as the smoke caught at the backs of their throats and went down into their lungs.

'Now!' he called. Without hesitation, he leapt forward into the smoke. Heat struck at his body worse than that of the midday sun in the desert. He was only vaguely aware of the others running with him, heads low, smoke swirling around them. A slug from one of the rear windows of the ranch laid a red-hot bar across his left arm as he ran forward. Thorpe fired several shots and a man fell out of the window, dimly-seen, blood on his shirt.

Reaching the door, Clem kicked it open with his boot and stormed inside, the gun in his hands roaring death. A couple of men stood beside the window on the far side of the room. They spun savagely as he burst in on them, guns flashing flame. He felt the bullets fan his cheek, then he was down on one knee, firing from the hip. He saw one of the men stumble forward, clawing at his chest. The other man tried to turn and run but stumbled over his companion's body, went down onto his face and tried desperately to pull himself upright. Behind Clem, Thorpe appeared in the doorway. He fired instantly and the man's eyes glazed as he fell forward, guns dropping from his nerveless fingers.

Swiftly, Clem glanced about him, taking in everything in an unfocussed stare. There were three other men lying at the backs of the windows, but none of them looked like Heller and he did not wait to examine them any further, but leapt for the stairs and ran up them two at a time, reaching the top and peering in front of him along the narrow corridor. He had the feeling that Heller was around here some-where, that he would not be down below now, risking his skin where death flew in every window and lanced across every room as more of the nesters came bursting into the ranch. From the rear, he heard the sound of confused shouting and guessed that the rest of the men had come rushing in. He checked the first room he came to, but it was empty and he passed quickly on to the next, guns ready, a strange tightness constricting the muscles of his throat and chest.

The door of the room was slightly ajar as he came up to it and he knew, by some strange instinct within him, that Heller was at the back of that door, waiting for him to enter, to shoot him in the back. He tightened his lips into a thin, hard line across the middle of his face. The conviction was so strong that he knew he was not mistaken.

Silently, he padded forward. Down below, the sound of gunfire rose to an ear-shattering crescendo. But here, there seemed to be an unearthly silence over everything, as if this part of the house were completely divorced from every other part. He imagined he could hear the other's heavy breathing at the back of the door. Reaching it, he suddenly lunged forward, throwing all of his weight against it. The door flew open and there was a loud cry as Heller was hurled into the middle of the room. He fell heavily against the small table and went over onto his back. Clem stood framed in the doorway, both guns out, his body filled with a blend of hatred and anger and triumph.

Heller squeezed the trigger of the Colt in his hand, but his aim was bad and the slug merely whined over Clem's shoulder and buried itself in the wooden upright of the door at his back.

Clem's guns barked and the Colt in Heller's hand flew across the room as he twisted over onto his side, clutching at his shattered wrist. Pain showed in his eyes, blended with a look of defeat. For a moment, he lay there, then struggled to his feet. His lips twisted as he came erect.

'Could be that you still don't recollect who I am,' Clem told him, watching him closely for the first wrong move. 'Probably you remember Sheriff Peterson back in Carson City, the man you shot in the back without giving him a chance to draw. That man was more than a father to me, Heller, and I swore I'd destroy his murderer and kill him myself.'

'Peterson. But I never knew that you — ' The look of realisation in the other's eyes, a sure admission of his guilt, was replaced a moment later by one of terror. Clem's words seemed to sink into his mind for the first time. He turned his head swiftly from side to side as though seeking a way of escape from that room. Slowly, he began to back away from the guns in Clem's hands as the other advanced towards him. 'I wanted you to know who it was who killed you — and why.' Clem grated thinly. His fingers grew bar-hard on the triggers, whitening with the exertion. His face was savage and fixed.

Wildly, Heller spun on his heel, still clutching at his bleeding wrist and it was this that proved his undoing.

Before Clem could stop him, the other had lurched backward, off-balanced. For a second, he remained there, outlined against the moonlight that flooded in through the shattered window. Then, arms waving madly, he toppled backward into the night, his last cries snatched away from his lips by the wind.

Clem went forward slowly and stared down, out of the window, into the courtyard below. Heller's body was just visible in the smoke which still swirled around the house. He lay face-downwards on the hard ground, arms outspread, his legs twisted beneath him. Clem did not have to look twice to know that the other was dead. And with him, had died the corrupted empire he had tried to build, one founded on terror and avarice and fear. It had come toppling down about him.

He went slowly down the stairs and found that the fighting in the ranch was over. Those of Heller's gunmen that hadn't been killed had given themselves up to the nesters. On the hill itself, the battle was still raging, but even here the sound of gunfire was dying down as the rustlers, realising that they had met a superior force, one far stronger than they had been led to believe would be ranged against them, began to flee.

Twenty minutes later, it was all over. The fire which had destroyed the bunkhouse, had spread rapidly to the ranch itself and the building was now a raging inferno. Constructed almost entirely of imported timber, it burned fiercely and as he sat in the saddle on top of the hill, looking down into the valley which had seen so much violence that night, Clem felt all of the anger and tension being washed from his body. He had set out to do what he had sworn to do, and now it was all finished. He holstered his guns slowly, knowing that he would not need to use them around here any more.

'That's about the end of that,' said Thorpe quietly. He seemed strangely subdued as he watched the magnificent ranch burn to the ground. 'A few of the rustlers got away so Bert says, heading into the desert. Reckon we'll have no trouble from them though. They'll keep on riding until they're over the border if they have any sense. Now that Heller is dead, there's nothing for them around this territory.'

Clem nodded. Down below, the roof of the ranch fell in with a roar and a gush of red-edged flame. Sparks licked up in a rising cloud towards the moon-flecked heavens. Very soon, there would be nothing left of the Heller ranch but an empty, blackened shell and a few memories. Perhaps, he thought wryly, that was how it ought to be.

He wheeled his horse and rode back with Thorpe and the other nesters to their camp on the outskirts of Senica. Things were better wiped out completely.

'Reckon you won't have to wait for a legal battle to claim your land, Brad,' he said an hour later, as he sat beside the fire with the others and tucked into a plate of stew. 'With Heller dead, there's nothing in your way. You can claim that land tomorrow. Should be real good land too. The railroad will be coming through Senica most any day now. Reckon this is going to grow into a mighty fine place someday.'

The other regarded him from beneath shaggy black brows. 'Figgering on staying around to see that day?' he asked soberly.

Clem shrugged. 'Ain't made up my mind what to do yet. I only came to these parts to kill Heller. Now that he's dead, don't see there's any reason for me to stay around. Could be I'll just ride on as far west as my sorrel will take me and find a new country somewhere out there.'

The other chewed on his food for a moment, then said reflectively, looking up at the moon, where it was lowering itself down towards the western horizon. 'Could be that even if you rode all the way to California, you'd just find

311

that every place you came to was no different to this that we have here. A man can lead a wandering life most of the time, but there comes a time when he had a hankering to stop, put down his roots and settle somewhere. That's why we came out here, to make a new home for ourselves and our families.

'It's a good country and I reckon I'll die happy here.' He got slowly to his feet. 'It'll soon be dawn and there's a lot we have to do tomorrow if we're to move in and stake our claims to that land.'

Beside the wagon, he paused, struck a match on the side and lit the pipe which he pulled from the pocket of his jacket.

'Think over what I've said Clem. Could be that you might find the answer over there by the spring.' He inclined his head towards the edge of the camp.

Clem grinned, then got to his feet. In spite of the weariness in his body, he doubted if he would sleep. He walked around the wagons and went over to the place where the small spring bubbled out of the rocks, turning the older man's words over in his mind. For the past few years, there had been a driving purpose in him, which had kept him moving from one place to another. Now that was gone and he felt there was nothing to take its place. He was a man without a purpose.

As he reached the spring, someone stepped out of the shadows among the small grove of trees and came noiselessly towards him. For a moment, he felt a brief surge of anger. He had come here with the desire to be alone, to try to think things out for himself, to decide on the best course open to him. Then he knew, with a sureness that he had never experienced before, that there was no need for him to think things out, that his answer was here, at the camp.

'I guessed you'd come back, Clem.' Zoe Thorpe came over and stood by him, looking out to the east where the first faint light of the new day was just beginning to show, touching the sky with a narrow band of gold. The stars overhead were beginning to fade slowly.

'I wanted to come back, Zoe,' he said hesitantly. 'But I wasn't sure that — ' He paused for a moment, saw her smiling up at him, and knew that everything was going to be all right. 'I reckon you've got to marry me, Zoe,' he said softly, 'or I'll have to ride out of camp and go on riding west until I get clear to the Pacific Ocean.'

'That would be too far to ride,' she agreed, laughing with him as the dawn brightened.

THE END

814 2655 615 840
Jaf 6 JANNET